Mindfulness and Murder

A Father Ananda Mystery

Nick Wilgus

Mindfulness and Murder

First published as paperback edition in 2003 by
Silkworm Books
This new and revised edition published in 2012 by

Crime Wave Press
Flat D, 11th Fl. Liberty Mansion
26E Jordan Road
Yau Ma Tei, Hong Kong
http://www.crimewavepress.com

ISBN: 978-988-16556-6-0

Cover photo from "Mindfulness and Murder"
directed by Tom Waller, courtesy of
© De Warrenne Pictures Co. Ltd. & D. Bertay.
www.dewarrenne.com
Vithaya Pansringarm appears as Father Ananda.

Quotations from the Dhammapada taken from
"What The Buddha Taught"
by Venerable Dr. W. Rahula, Haw Trai Foundation
Bangkok, 1995.

CHAPTER ONE

"There is no fire like lust. There is no grip like hate.
There is no net like delusion.
There is no river like craving."

The Lord Buddha. From the Dhammapada, #251.

One

"Ananda, come with me."

The abbot took hold of my arm and pulled me along the concrete footpath in the darkness.

"What's wrong?" I asked.

He offered a strangled smile, but wouldn't reply.

It was just after four in the morning, and the monastery was waking up, having been roused by the sound of the temple gong. Monks were beginning to straighten up their kutis, or tend to their morning business in the communal bathrooms. The temple dogs howled and barked, whether in annoyance at having been woken, or in anticipation of breakfast, no one really knew — breakfast would not be for another three hours, so perhaps it was a combination of both.

We followed the footpath that led toward the back of the monastery grounds and came to a stop before a long disused bathroom, just a few meters from the wall that separated our monastery grounds from the soon-to-be-busy world of the city of Bangkok, which lay just beyond.

The abbot was agitated. His large body trembled and his small eyes were rather wild. During my eight years at Wat Mahanat, I had never seen him in such a state.

"What is it?" I asked again, perplexed — he was acting as if someone had been murdered.

"In there!" he exclaimed, pointing to the bathroom.

I looked through the half-open door and saw the bottoms of feet set at a rather unnatural angle.

The air was heavy with a familiar, unpleasant smell — the smell of death. I had been a police officer, years ago, before I had taken to the robes of a Buddhist monk, and that smell was only too familiar.

Someone had indeed been murdered, or at the very least, was dead. As if I was still a police officer and had just been summoned to a crime scene, I began to look around, to survey the scene.

The abbot handed me his flashlight. "Ananda, take a look.

I was going to, but first I trained the light on the ground to either side of the concrete footpath, wanting to see if there were any footprints in the dirt. The concrete walkway ended at the bathroom itself. The grounds nearby were covered with large trees heavy with leaves, but there was not much grass to speak of. Next to the bathroom, there was none at all.

"You haven't been walking around, off the footpath?" I asked.

The abbot shook his head.

"Are you sure? It's important."

"No!" he exclaimed impatiently.

"How did you discover the body?" I asked. What had he been doing out here in the dark, when the best bathroom was right next to his own kuti, which was in the completely opposite direction?

"I was walking," he said distractedly, bunching his hands together. "Doing a meditation. I haven't been sleeping well lately. Just take a look now, would you, Ananda, before every-one wakes up and wants to know what's going on."

I went to the door and pushed it all the way open. The bare feet were clearly visible from where we stood in the en-tryway. I fumbled around on the wall for the light switch, eventually found it and flicked the light on. The dust on the floor, I saw right away, had been disturbed. I was careful to step around the prints as I went through the small entryway and into the bathroom itself. The smell was much stronger inside and it took me a moment to adjust. The smell brought back suddenly vivid memories of other days, of other scenes. To my right were two stalls. In front of me was a large sink. To my left was an open shower. In the corner of the shower was a large water jar, the sort that water is stored in, either for bathing or manually flushing a toilet. It was about waist-high, a meter across.

In this particular water jar was either a man or an older teenage boy, lying across the lip of it. And whoever this particular fellow was, he was decidedly dead. The smell alone told me as much.

It had been a long time since I'd seen a dead body, and it took me a moment to get my nerves settled. As a police officer, I had learned the invaluable art of being detached in the face of tragedy, of not identifying with the victim, not thinking of the victim as a person but rather an object, a thing to be investigated, probed, the circumstances of his death a puzzle to be figured out. It was a way to shield oneself from the reality of just how brutal we humans can be to each other, what lengths we will go to, the pain we're capable of inflicting on each other. If I thought too much about these things, I would lose my nerve, so I pushed them all from my mind and concentrated on the task at hand, making a mental list of notes.

The victim was nude. The head, shoulders, chest and arms were inside the water jar. The rest of the body was not. The feet were resting on the floor, toes curled, bottoms facing outward. I moved closer to the body, steeling my stomach against the smell. I put a hand on the fellow's hip. He was cold, but not overly so. I bent to examine his feet, lifting one to look at the toenails, then looking carefully at the floor. I did not see any scratches, either on the floor or on the toe nails, suggesting there had been no struggle – if the victim had been pushed, face-down, into the jar of water in an attempt to drown him, he would have kicked out, trying to gain leverage on the floor to free himself. At the very least, water would have been spilled. I saw no signs of such a struggle. The foot itself came up easily, which meant that rigor mortis had passed. This, in turn, meant the poor fellow had been dead for a day or more – while bodies become stiff with rigor mortis soon after death, this phase passes after a day or so.

The bottoms of the feet were clean, which suggested he had either been wearing shoes – there were none to be seen – or he had been carried here. Just as there were no shoes, there were no clothes to be seen, and that also said something about what had happened here and why. To force someone to remove their clothes before killing them was suggestive of many things: Sex, obviously, but also an intention to humiliate, or frighten the victim, or to increase the feeling of vulnerability. It's hard to fight back or feel confident about yourself when you're nude and as physically vulnerable as you can possibly get, especially if the murder weapon is a knife or a sharp object like a razor blade.

Although I could not tell for certain, and wouldn't be able to until the body was removed from the water, the victim seemed of average height and size, a bit on the thin size, with no tattoos or other distinguishing marks, at least none that I could see. His skin tone was light, suggesting that he might be from the North, from a city like Chiang Mai. The blush of youth was on the skin, which meant the man was probably in his early twenties, perhaps even younger.

I looked at the right arm, lifting it slightly away from the water to get a better view of the crux of the elbow. Needle marks were clearly visible. Had one of our monks been in the habit of injecting drugs?

A bit of unease settled into my belly. I didn't want this person to be one of my fellow monks, and I most certainly didn't want it to be one of the boys in our homeless youth program – yet there was youthfulness about the body that suggested this might be so.

Without disturbing the body, there wasn't much else I could do but suggest the abbot call the police. I went back outside and told him as much.

"This is going to be trouble, isn't it, Ananda?" he asked, scowling.

"Probably not as much trouble for you as it was for him," I replied.

Two

Lt. Somchai from the Silom Police Station located not far from the Wat Mahanat monastery complex arrived about thirty minutes later with three of his men. He was courteous, offering a wai gesture of respect to both the abbot and myself. He was somewhere in his forties and had a smoking-induced cough. The polluted streets of Bangkok probably didn't help his lungs any more than his chain-smoking did.

"Ananda was once a police officer," the abbot said straight away. "He can be your liaison." The abbot then excused himself – there was a monastery to run, after all, and more than 200 monks to oversee, not to mention our youth program which housed about forty homeless boys, and our boarding school for grade school kids. But I knew the abbot was simply squeamish and in no hurry to deal with a dead body.

"I had a preliminary look," I told Somchai, motioning toward the bathroom. "The victim is face down in a large water jar. There are footprints in the dust on the floor that your men should photograph. I did not see any footprints around the bathroom itself. Aside from that, there isn't anything else I can tell you."

"Do you know who the victim is?"

I shook my head.

Somchai ordered his photographer to take pictures of the bathroom floor, and then of the body itself. Another one of his men marked off the crime scene with yellow tape. Somchai took some time, watching over these preparations, puffing on a cigarette.

"I should quit these," he said, holding the cigarette up and looking at it. "Nasty things."

"Yes you should," I replied. "And yes they are."

He offered a resigned smile.

In the distance, through the trees, I could see monks beginning to congregate, wanting to know what was going on.

"Perhaps you'd like to assist," Somchai asked, stubbing out his cigarette.

They were preparing to move the body and do an examination.

I wasn't certain, but my curiosity had been aroused. I wanted to know who the victim was. I wanted a chance to examine the rest of the body. And I was concerned that such a thing as this could happen at the monastery I called home. So I followed Somchai into the bathroom. One of his men, wearing latex gloves, gripped the body by the shoulders and pulled it out of the water, allowing the victim to slide down and come to a rest on the floor in somewhat of a heap.

I winced.

It was one of our homeless boys – Nong Noi, if I remembered the name correctly. It seemed to me that he was about seventeen years old and had come to the temple trying to beat a drug addiction. I conducted meditation classes for kids trying to kick their habits cold turkey, and it was always a trying experience. There were usually three or four of them, and we would sit down together in a circle, and I would find myself being watched by haunted eyes as they struggled to stop trembling and shaking for even as little as five minutes. Nong Noi had been one of those boys, and whatever habit he'd had was certainly kicked now.

That wasn't the worst of it. His eyes had been gouged out and a fat yellow candle, the sort we burned in front of the Buddha statue in the main temple, had been stuffed into his mouth. The jaw was set at such an unnatural angle that it must have certainly been broken. In addition, there appeared to be cigarette burns on his chest – about six of them, small circles of burned flesh.

Somchai grimaced and turned his face away.

I did likewise.

"I think we can safely assume it wasn't suicide," he said.

Precisely. But who would want to murder one of our boys. And why?

Three

I squatted next to Somchai as he examined the body. I looked at the boy's fingernails, the insides of his elbows, his neck, his face, the scalp, his back, his legs. Aside from the obvious wounds, we saw no others. The light bulb overhead cast garish shadows. The body seemed unnaturally pale, as if drained of blood.

For the first few minutes, I was all right, feeling appropriately detached and calm. Yet the sight of the boy's body reminded me of the sight of another such body, and a strange sort of grief took hold of me, taking me many years back into the past, to another crime scene. The body I had seen that day belonged to a thirteen-year-old boy. He was sitting in the front seat of a Toyota. The white of his school uniform was red with blood, and more blood trickled down his face from the bullet hole in his forehead. His mother had gotten out of the car and was opening the gate to their small home when a gunman on the back of a motorcycle had pulled up and shot her, and then her son. I could still see her lying on the ground, face down, hair in the gutter. At the time, I was struck by the horrible unfairness of it all, shocked by how violent we could be, the lengths we could go to when settling a score or taking care of business.

What I had seen that day haunted me down through the years.

I stood up and took my eyes away from Nong Noi's body, suddenly feeling faint and unwell. Hadn't I taken to the robes partly to get away from these death scenes, my mind no longer able to cope with them, my faith in humanity all but shattered?

"You all right?" Somchai asked, looking up to me from the other side of the body.

"Out of practice," I said, trying to smile.

"Understandable," the man said kindly.

I looked once more at the body, trying to focus, to find that detachment I had started with, and had worked so hard, during my years in the robes, to nourish.

Nong Noi. He was familiar to me, but then again there were so many boys coming and going and I had long ago lost track of them all. So many names, stories, heartaches. So many pairs of eyes looking at you, as if somehow you could save them, as if you had something they desperately needed, and it was only a matter of you be willing to give it to them. Was it love? I didn't know. I was no longer capable of love. Compassion, yes. Love, no — it hurt too much and reminded me of too many things I hoped to forget.

It was a womanly thing to feel, but I wanted to take this dead boy into my arms, cradle him, tell him everything would be all right, that this madness would soon be over, that he would wake and discover it had all been a horrible dream. I wanted to cover the boy's nakedness, cover his gouged out eyes. I had the insane thought that if I could find his gouged out eyes and put them back, that this would somehow make it better.

Nothing was ever going to be better for this boy, not in this life.

"I'm going to take the candle out of his mouth," Somchai said, as if to warn me.

I watched, trying to be impassive.

He took hold of it, pulled it, met with resistance. The boy's teeth had sunk into the wax. When he pulled, the boy's head was raised up off the floor, and his wet hair fell about his face and ears, dripping water.

"Do you think he was choked to death?" I asked. I was finding it hard to breathe and could hardly get the words out. I imagined this boy, in my mind's eye, with this large candle shoved down his throat, choking and gagging. If his killer had pinched his nostrils shut, he would have been desperate for air, desperate to breathe. It would have been a silent death — no chance to scream, to cry out, to hurl one last invective at the world.

Somchai pulled on the candle again, grunted, eventually managed to work it loose, the boy's head flopping back on the tiles when he did so.

"I don't know if he choked. I don't know what to think, to be honest," he said.

He retrieved a rectal thermometer from his bag, inserted it. Bodies cooled at a certain rate, so many degrees per hour. To ascertain a more exact time of death was therefore sometimes just a matter of doing the arithmetic.

"I would say twenty-four to thirty hours," Somchai said, looking up to me. "At some point on Monday night."

It was now Wednesday morning.

The body had been here all day yesterday and no one had noticed.

Four

The sun rose, the monks went on their alms rounds in the surrounding neighborhoods, returned and ate their breakfasts.

I kept vigil at the death scene.

Monks began to congregate, wanting to see what was happening. Vendors began to appear too. Word spread, and quickly, and soon there were all sorts of people standing around, looking at the boy's naked, defiled body with its sightless eyes. Somchai's men had carried the body out of the bathroom and left it lying on the concrete walkway.

Photographers from the dailies showed up, tipped off, no doubt, by someone in the police department. I was enraged to see their flashbulbs popping and cameras whirring. Every day the newspapers printed the most gruesome pictures they could find on their front pages — decapitated bodies, murdered prostitutes, body parts strewn around after an accident, suicides, drownings, workers chopped in half by machinery. The more lurid it was, the more newspapers they sold, and if family members woke up one day and saw a cherished loved one displayed in such a fashion on the front pages, who cared about their feelings? There were papers to sell.

Lt. Somchai and his men had done what they could, which was, admittedly, not that much. They had photographed the scene, taken some tissue samples, and searched the immediate area. Now there was a monastery of more than 200 monks to interview, not to mention dozens of teenage boys — each and every one a potential suspect. It would take a lot more time and resources than Somchai had to properly investigate Nong Noi's death.

His eyes seemed to be telling me this as he took my arm and led me away from the others to a place beneath the sprawling trees where we could talk privately.

"You were once a police officer," he said, "so you know how it is. I've done what I can do here. I'll interview some of the monks. But we're talking about a homeless boy who's gotten himself killed, and I'm not going to be able to devote a lot of time to this case. I hope you understand."

I understood only too well. There were a limited number of resources available to the police department in Bangkok. The police force, as a general rule, was not very well trained. Officers had to buy their own uniforms, their own guns. They were poorly paid. They did not have access to all the latest developments in forensic science and investigative procedures. They could not send off samples of DNA to a lab for testing, the way they did in Western movies — the expense prohibited this in all but the most important cases. The police did the best they could with what little they had, relying mostly on gut feelings, past experience, and what little training they had received.

Somchai was telling me upfront that Nong Noi was probably going to slip through the cracks, that there were more important matters requiring his attention than a dead homeless boy.

"I could assist you," I said, not really wanting to do any such thing — I had taken to the robes of a Buddhist monk partly as a way to get away from all the dead bodies and violence and the human viciousness my eyes had seen. I was in no hurry to go back to it. I didn't miss it. After eight years as a monk, I had finally achieved a state of calm and tranquility, and was in no hurry to jeopardize my efforts. Yet my mouth continued on, as if it had a mind of its own. "I can interview the monks and the boys," I said, strengthening my case. "I can follow up leads. I might have an easier time of it than you, since you're an outsider."

He offered a small, embarrassed smile. "It would be easier for you, that's true. You can poke around this monastery in places I could not."

He rubbed the back of his neck with his right hand, making a face. Then he fished out his pack of cigarettes from his back pocket and lit one up, taking a deep drag. "This boy has obviously been murdered. That's pretty self-evident. Now we don't have any footprints around the bathroom, in the dirt areas, and that tells me that he wasn't brought over that wall there" — he pointed to the back wall just a few meters from where we stood, taking another drag on his cigarette. "It's possible your killer brought the body over that wall and dumped it in this bathroom, but not likely. He could have swept the dirt behind him to get rid of his tracks, but then we would be able to tell that the dirt had been swept. So that leaves me with one conclusion — that whoever put this body in that bathroom came down this concrete walkway. In other words, it was one of your monks, or someone from inside this complex."

There was no arguing with his logic.

"So you'd really help?" he asked, offering me a hopeful look.

I found myself nodding, committing myself to a course of action that I might regret.

"And what about the body?" he asked.

I looked over to where Nong Noi had been laid. "We'll take care of it."

Lt. Somchai gave me his business card and offered a respectful wai, telling me to call on him if I needed any assistance tracking down leads, or any assistance at all that he might be able to render. He seemed almost apologetic to be leaving the case in my hands. I told him I would stop by for copies of the photographs of the footprints in the bathroom — that was one lead I could follow up. He agreed, and then he and his men left, as did most of the press and the other onlookers.

He was a good man, I thought. He was being honest about his limitations, and what could reasonably be expected of the situation. The plain fact was that any given police station's cases were ranked according to priority. And priority, in Bangkok, had to do with money, wealth and status. Those on the low end of the spectrum weren't likely to receive full, complete investigations. And if you were homeless boy with no family to call your own, well, what did it matter anyway? If a bit of riff-raff trash came to a bad end, it was probably the victim's fault — why bother figuring out all the sordid details? There was no reward for solving such cases, or investing resources in them.

Yet every death deserved respect, every victim deserved justice, no matter how far down the economic spectrum that victim might be.

I had asked Brother Suchinno, our monastery's maintenance man, to bring sheets. He was standing next to the body now, holding the sheets and waiting for me. Together we spread a sheet on the ground and put the body on it. From the corner of my eye, I saw a lone photographer crouching opposite from me by the monastery wall, snapping away. Furious, I got to my feet and charged after the young man, my pent-up anger fixated on a concrete target.

Suchinno caught hold of my orange robes.

"Ananda, don't," he said, trying to turn me away from the photographer.

I shook my arm free and stalked off. The photographer grabbed up his gear and fled. Given our reputation for calm indifference, I suppose he hadn't expected to see an angry monk ready to rip the film right out of his camera and cram it down his throat.

It wasn't very monk-like behavior, but I had my reasons.

Five

Brother Suchinno and his assistants, Brother Chittasangwaro and Brother Salisangwaro, carried Nong Noi's body to the death room, where bodies were prepared for funerals. As this building was always locked, they had to set the body down and wait for Suchinno to fetch the key.

Once inside, Brother Suchinno took charge — this was his territory. I helped as best I could. We bathed Nong Noi, washing his limbs, rinsing out his hair, wiping away the bloodstains from his cheeks, dabbing at the edges of his eyes — I think we were all unnerved by the absence of them, by those gaping sockets.

I often meditated on death, as a way to prepare for it, as did most Buddhist monks. But the fact of it — its coldness, the rubberiness of the skin, the lifelessness of the corpse, the way the body smells, decays, breaks down, the utter absence of life, vitality, spark — the reality of it was always sobering. And the death of a child was harder to accept, to make sense of.

The teachings of the Lord Buddha are comprised of the Four Noble Truths, and it was the first of these that I was thinking about, the truth about suffering. A simple observation, but very true. Birth is suffering, aging, sickness, death are suffering. To not get what one wants, to be united with that which is unpleasant, to live in poor conditions, to yearn and long for and never obtain — all create suffering. It's the recognition of this truth that forms the basis of everything the Buddha taught.

Nong Noi suffered. I saw it reflected in his sightless eyes, in the burns on his breast, in the needle marks on his arms. There's physical suffering, but also mental suffering, which is sometimes worse. What sort of suffering had led him to inject drugs? Had led him to our homeless program in the first place? Had led him to the person who had killed him?

We wrapped his body in a winding sheet and moved it to the place where it would lie in state until that evening, when it would be placed inside a coffin and taken to one of the salas for the funeral rites.

I washed up and left the death room, feeling agitated and unsettled by that morning's goings-on.

There were times when I didn't feel much like a monk. This was one of those times. I was burning inside with a curious sort of anger and disgust with the world, with its injustices, with the fact that it so often offered tragedy to those least able to cope with it. I suppose I was also feeling a bit sorry for myself and for my monastery — we were supposed take care of these boys, not get them murdered. And I had also been reminded that although I could leave the world, it would still find me.

The first thing I needed to do, if I was going to investigate his death, was to find out everything I could about Nong Noi: His friends, his background, his history, who he talked to, with whom he was close. This would give me some indication of what had led him to his death, or who might have been responsible for it.

I went to the main office and asked the secretary, a young monk named Brother Kittisaro, for Nong Noi's file. Kittisaro had it on his desk already and handed it to me — he was nothing if not efficient. A good-looking man on the late side of his twenties, he wore wire rim glasses that made him seem a bit bookish. There was, about his features, something delicate and refined. He was also very short, and had long ago become immune to our good-natured ribbing over his stature.

"How are those computers coming?" I asked him, my mind in need of a distraction. He was our resident computer geek, and I suspected he spent more time figuring out how computers worked than he did typing correspondence for the abbot.

"I'm going to install Linux on one of these machines," he said proudly, giving me a goofy grin.

Linux? That sounded like a disease. I made to face to suggest that whatever he was talking about was completely over my head, hoping he wouldn't try to explain what it was. "Can you get someone to cover my meditation class this afternoon?" I asked.

He nodded.

I flipped through Nong Noi's file. His real name was Chaiwat Lertsuwan — his nickname was Nong Noi.

"There's nothing listed here for this parents," I said, giving Kittisaro a glance.

He shrugged. "They don't often want to list their parents. The abbot says to let it go. Some of the kids are afraid they'll be tracked down, afraid their parents will find out where they are. With some of the horror stories I've heard, I understand perfectly. Sometimes the last thing these kids want is to be sent home."

I bit at my lower lip. Most of the kids that washed up on our shores came from broken homes and had experienced all sorts of abuse, violence, neglect. They had been beaten, molested, kicked out. Many were orphans. Some were disabled. Some had psychological problems. All were what we liked to call "at risk" — we had developed a whole vocabulary to talk about kids falling through the cracks of our society.

Nong Noi was originally from a village called Wiang Chai up near Chiang Rai in the far North, a rather long way away. It did not appear that he had finished high school. There were reports about his anti-social, rather unfriendly behavior. He was clearly not the sort of child that played well with others. One report described his behavior as "erratic, withdrawn, a bit of a temper. Not very friendly."

"We have to notify the family," I said.

Kittisaro nodded. "But how? I've been trying, and I'll keep at it, but they may not have a phone. He may not have a family at all, for that matter."

"Do your best," I said. "I hate to take you away from the Lunar thing, but I'm going to need to see the files for all our boys in the homeless program, the current ones."

He nodded. "It's Linux, by the way."

"Of course," I said.

Six

I went back to see Brother Suchinno. He was our all-around fixer-upper and keeper-upper, and there didn't seem to be a machine or gadget he couldn't pry apart and put back together in working order. He was about my age, pushing fifty, and plain spoken. His trim, compact body hadn't an ounce of fat anywhere to be seen, and his arms and legs were ropy with muscle. He never seemed to worry about anything more than leaky toilets or broken fans.

"I need some more help," I said, going into his workroom where I found him hunched over the innards of a toaster which the kitchen had just sent over for him to fix.

He gave me an inquisitive glance. Suchinno wasn't known for using words unless he had to.

"Afraid it won't be pleasant," I said. "We need to go through the trash."

His shaved eyebrows went up.

"Yes, the trash. All of it. And right away, before any of it gets thrown out."

"We're doing this because ..."

"Because I need to find that boy's clothes," I answered.

"That poor boy," he said, shaking his head.

"He was nude," I said. "That means his clothes have to be somewhere. So the first thing we have to do is look through the trash. If that doesn't turn up anything, we'll have to search the whole complex, and that will take a lot longer."

He nodded, pushing away his work and getting to his feet. "I'll get my assistants. I'll meet you out by the Dumpsters. I assume you want to do it now?"

I did.

I went out to the Dumpsters and waited for him, and he arrived quickly with his two young assistants, Chittasangwaro and Salisangwaro.

"We're looking for clothes," I said to them. "Probably stuffed in a bag, toward the bottom."

Although monks wear up to three robes, most often we wear two, and when working, only one, the inner robe, which is like a sarong and secured around the waist with a flat belt that can be tied up with its two cords. The upper robe is also much like a sarong, and is most often worn by putting one end on the left shoulder and then bringing the other around, under the right armpit, and over the left shoulder as well. When the weather turns cold, a third robe, the outer robe, can also be worn over the shoulders. For the job we had to do now, we laid aside our upper robes and gathered up the bottoms of the inner robes so as not to get them dirty. There were two Dumpsters. Suchinno and Chittasangwaro tackled one, leaving the other for Salisangwaro and myself.

I climbed into the Dumpster with Salisangwaro, who did not look like he was going to enjoy this any more than I was. The Dumpsters had been emptied on Monday morning. It was now Wednesday, and there were blessedly few bags to contend with — our Dumpster was only half full. Even so, it was a smelly job and I was afraid I was going to be bitten by a rat, or worse. Who knew what could be lurking in the bottom of these Dumpsters? I was afraid to speculate. I opened bags and poked through them with a long stick, somewhat astonished at our refuse output.

About an hour into this exercise, Brother Suchinno called out.

"I think I found something," he said, looking over the lip of his Dumpster.

I crawled out of my own Dumpster and went over to stand in front of his. He tossed down a small black bag, which had been stuffed inside another bag, the large sort we used for the public bins. Along with wadded up pieces of newspaper, there was a white tank top and black pair of shorts. The tank top was bloody.

"Those belong to that boy?" Salisangwaro asked, jumping out of the Dumpster and looking at me.

I nodded.

"Do you know who did it?"

I shook my head.

"Well, I hope you catch him," Salisangwaro said, a dark look in his eyes. He had a large Buddha image hanging from a chain around his neck, lying against his bare chest. He brought this to his lips and kissed it. "Not that I bear him any ill will, of course."

Not that I did either.

I carried the bag back to my kuti. I didn't want to go through it, but I had to. I spread the contents out on the ground, first straightening up some of the newspaper to lay the clothes on and wrap them up properly. The tank top was indeed bloody, stiff and stuck together in spots. I didn't disturb it. The shorts had two pockets in the front. I looked through them, but found nothing. There was another pocket on the back, and now I got lucky: inside was a business card for a reporter from the Thai Rath newspaper.

I fetched an envelope and put the card inside it, leaving it in my kuti. I gathered the clothes up, wrapping them in paper and putting them inside another plastic bag. I dug around some more in the black bag, because there were two other items that were missing, which I wasn't sure I wanted to find: Nong Noi's eyeballs.

I had never been called upon in my life to dispose of two eyeballs, but if I had to, I suppose I would flush them down the nearest toilet — that would be the only way I could be sure that no one would find them.

I searched the bag thoroughly but they were not there, for which I sighed gratefully. If the killer had bunched all these papers up, then he had undoubtedly left a lot of fingerprints for us to find, unless, he course, he had been smart enough to wear gloves. I hoped he hadn't been.

When I was finished, I took my towel and went to the communal bath to wash the stink of garbage off my body. Then I took the bags to the main office, where Kittisaro gave me a searching look.

"I need to store these somewhere," I said. "They're evidence, so they need to be locked away."

"A bag of garbage is evidence?" he asked, turning up his nose at the smell.

"You'd be surprised what turns up in the trash these days."

Kittisaro opened the storeroom. Inside it was a large iron cage that could be padlocked, in which valuable items were stored.

"Who has the keys to this?" I asked.

"I do," Kittisaro said. "And probably Brother Suchinno."

"Let's put this in there. But I want all the keys. Can you get them for me?"

We stored the bags and he handed over his key to the padlock, promising to get Suchinno's, which I could pick up when I was ready. I did not believe the shirt and short would be of much use — it would be difficult to have them properly analyzed — but I wanted them to be on hand should I need them at some point in the future. If I actually did catch Nong Noi's killer, I would need all the evidence I could get.

Seven

I walked through the maze of buildings over to the dormitory, which housed more than a hundred monks as well as our youth program. Brother Khantiphalo was in charge of the homeless teens project, and I found him in the dorm with the kids, folding and putting away piles of laundry. He saw me coming and set aside what he was doing — sorting through a mountain of socks.

"Father Ananda," he said by way of greeting.

"I need to see Nong Noi's things, Khantiphalo."

"Of course. I thought someone might, so I set them aside already."

He led me through the dorm and out the main door. His office was the next door down, a small, cramped affair piled high with papers and an odd assortment of footballs, badminton rackets, nets, books and whatnot — the sort of things to keep teenage boys occupied.

Khantiphalo was a large fellow, about thirty-five, a bit of a bull dog, broad shouldered, round faced, strong. He was not the sort of person the kids could wrap around their fingers. He was very much in charge, and very much the boss, and yet also a gentle person with heaps of patience and understanding of the human condition. That he had tackled the youth program and had done quite well made him nothing less than a saint in our eyes. Taking care of these boys with their problems, hang-ups and sometimes violent natures was not at all easy.

He'd walked in the boys' shoes himself, during his own childhood. Khantiphalo had taken to the robes at the early age of thirteen in order to get an education. Upon completion of his studies, he had decided that he liked the homeless life so much that he wanted to stay in the robes indefinitely.

There was a small box on his desk, and he handed it to me. "All of his belongings are in there," he said quietly.

"What can you tell me about him?" I asked, looking through the box.

He moved to clean off a seat so I could sit down, but I told him not to bother.

"Well," he said, rubbing at his jaw, "he wasn't very well liked. I'll tell you that straight off. He was troublesome. The other kids didn't want to be around him. Couldn't get along with anyone. That sort of stuff. I didn't think too much about it because he came from a messy background. Dad was an alcoholic. Mother was a bit off her rocker. They had too many kids, couldn't support them. Were abusive, rather mean, from what I could tell.

"Nong Noi got himself involved with drugs, hanging out with the wrong sort, drifting from place to place. After he came to Bangkok, he started hanging out at Lumphini Park, tricking, trying to make money to buy his drugs. I thought he might be gay, but I couldn't say for sure and he denied it, the one time I asked — I wasn't giving him a hard time about it, I was just trying to figure him out, see what I could do to help him. But he got real angry about me even so much as asking, so I didn't pursue it. Anyway, we get a lot of boys going through here who go that route — selling their bodies — not because they like it, but it's a quick way to make money. A lot of them get themselves hooked on drugs and need money and don't care what they have to do to get it."

He sighed. "Anyway, he was a real mess, is what I'm saying. Had a lot of pain inside. Lashed out at others. Impossible to live with or get along with. We were trying to help him, as best we could, but it wasn't easy. I mean, some of these kids you can reach — you can help them — and some of them you can't. They're just too damaged, and unless they remain with the program for a long time, we don't have enough contact to make any real difference."

I considered all of this for long moments. Brother Khantiphalo had just provided a whole slate of motives as to why someone would have wanted to kill this boy — he was troublesome, not well liked, hard to get along with, involved with the wrong sorts of people, of questionable morals and habits.

"Did anyone dislike him enough to kill him?" I asked.

Khantiphalo frowned. "I've been thinking about that myself. I don't know what to tell you. He got into fights, at times, with some of the other boys. But I don't know if that was enough for someone to want to kill him. I guess I don't know, to be honest. Maybe yes, maybe no. I mean, kids fight all the time, but they don't generally kill each other, do they?"

Fortunately no.

"Do you have any idea how we could contact his family?" I asked.

Khantiphalo shook his large head. "I think the father died already. The mother? I don't know. He wouldn't talk about her."

I thanked him and took the box and left.

I went back to the main office, and used one of Kittisaro's desks to spread out Noi's things. There were clothes, a hairbrush, cigarette lighters, plus a wad of papers banded together with a rubber band. I looked through these. There was a business card from Brother Khantiphalo, with the homeless center's hours written down on the back. There was another business card from an establishment that looked to be a bar — "Darllings" — with the name "Jo" written on the back. There were old lottery ticket stubs. There were notes with names and phone numbers. On one piece of paper was an address for a place in Bangkok, along with the inscription, "Jut and her husband." It was written in such a way as to suggest Jut might be his sister — I was going to have to pay her a visit and see for myself.

But the one piece of paper that interested me the most had been written on monastery stationery. It said:

Stop bothering me or else. "A."

If that wasn't a death threat, what was?

But who was "A"?

Eight

It was now about 11 a.m. and I was hungry.

We had our main meal early in the morning, after returning from the alms rounds. Technically, we were not to go on alms rounds until one could distinguish the lines on the palm of one's hand. We ate our main meal when we returned. We could also have another, smaller meal, before 12 p.m., but after that no solid food could be taken.

I had missed the main meal this morning and was now quite hungry indeed. I went to the dining hall for a small lunch, which I ate in silence, sitting in a circle with other senior monks, including Brother Thammarato, my mentor.

Of all the monks at the temple, Brother Thammarato was my favorite. We weren't supposed to have favorites, of course: That was the ideal. But I did. And so did everyone else.

Thammarato was my senior in age by about fifteen years, and had been in the monkhood since the age of twelve — almost fifty years. Almost my whole life. He was very learned in the Buddhist sutras and in advanced meditation techniques, yet one would never know it from the way he acted. A man in his sixties now, he was ever eager to politely laugh and joke, not above kicking a soccer ball around with the boys, not above talking to the chickens and scratching the dogs, not above helping out in the kitchen and persuading the kitchen help to cook up his favorites. Brother Thammarato was loved by all, and it was often whispered that he should be the abbot, and I thought perhaps one day he would be.

For me, the friendship stemmed from the fact that it was Brother Thammarato who had taken me in, and who had taught me how to meditate, and who had nursed me through the grief that had brought me to the monastery in the first place.

After our lunch, I needed to confess a fault, a practice particular to monastic life. Younger monks confessed their faults, sometimes two or three times a day, to a senior monk, who would, in turn, confess his own faults, if any, to the younger monk. Not all monks were in the habit of doing this, but it was a useful way to tackle bad habits.

I walked with Brother Thammarato to his kuti, where he sat down on the steps and regarded me patiently. We'd played out this ritual on many an occasion over the years.

"Elder Brother, I need to confess a fault," I said, seating myself before him, and offering the appropriate gestures of respect.

He waited patiently, regarding me with warm eyes.

"This morning I was quite angry," I said. "I saw photographers taking pictures of the dead boy's body, and I even chased after one. Of course, I didn't intend to be angry, and I did not attach to it or try in any way to nurse it, but still I was surprised by it, and it's obvious my temper hasn't completely been abandoned."

He offered a smile in response to this. Most of my confessions were about my temper. I had made a great deal of progress, it was true, and yet it was all too easy for me to slip into an angry state of mind.

As a monk, I was bound to the Pattimokkha, the 227 rules of conduct. Most of the offenses listed therein can be "expiated" by confessing them to a senior monk. All of these rules are designed to encourage good behavior, respectable behavior, behavior that reins in the senses and keeps the monk focused on the goal of enlightenment. On each full moon, we gather in the temple and recite the Patimokkha in full as a way to keep the rules fresh in our minds.

"It's good that you are careful about this matter," Thammarato said. "Still, perhaps you should ask yourself why the sight of the photographers made you angry."

I had been doing just that; I knew precisely why. Thammarato offered a sly smile as if to suggest that he knew precisely why as well.

"All these years, Ananda," he said softly. "All these years. But still ..."

Still.

"There are things I can't forget," I said.

"*Can't*? Or *won't*?"

"Can't," I said.

"*Won't*," he replied. "Don't kid yourself, Ananda. We've had this conversation before."

Indeed we had.

I took my leave of him and went to the main office to report to Abbot Worathammo to explain what I had found that morning and what I was doing. The abbot listened to me patiently, but was clearly waiting for the chance to interrupt.

"What is it?" I asked, curious.

"It seems that one of our brothers has gone missing," he said. "Brother Banditto. He hasn't been seen since yesterday morning, wasn't there for this morning's chanting, isn't in his cell, hasn't been seen today at all, hasn't signed out to go anywhere."

I bit at my lower lip. "That's very interesting, of course."

The abbot chuckled. "If I didn't know better, I would say he fled the scene."

"You think he's our killer?"

"Makes perfect sense, doesn't it? He kills the boy, gets cold feet, flees the scene. That's how it's done, isn't it?"

Indeed it was. But in general, monks didn't kill homeless boys, and if that's what had happened, we needed to know why and put the matter to rest. "You don't know for sure that he killed the boy," I pointed out. It could be dangerous to make that sort of assumption and give the real killer time to cover his tracks — and perhaps kill again.

"No, we don't know for sure," he admitted. "But anyway, keep it in mind. He may show up, of course, but I doubt it. And whether he does or not, we still need to know what happened to that boy. If it happens again, we're going to be in real trouble."

"But there's another reason why we have to get to the bottom of this," I said.

The abbot looked up.

The Patimokkha says there are four things which a monk can do which will result in his "defeat" — his instant, immediate defrocking. The first to have sexual intercourse, "even with a female animal." The others are stealing goods above a certain value, claiming supernatural powers that one does not possess, or taking the life of another person.

"If Banditto didn't kill this boy, then we have a monk walking around here in orange robes who is no longer a monk, and we are duty-bound to find him and expose him and expel him from the order — among other things."

"You're quite right," the abbot said.

Nine

The Wat Mahanat monastery and temple complex was a large, sprawling affair. The larger buildings were up in front, near the main road with its heavy traffic congestion and nauseating fumes. There was the temple, where we congregated for morning and evening chants, and in which our main Buddha image was enshrined. Next to the temple was the large sala, or meeting hall, where dharma instructions on the Lord Buddha's teachings were given and where public festivals were held. It was a large, open-air pavilion, rather larger than the temple. A series of smaller salas were strewn about, used mostly for funerals — we called them funeral halls. The main dormitory was also up in front, where the younger monks had their quarters, along with the large dormitory for our homeless teens program, and the boarding school for the younger boys. Also up in front were the laundry, the main office where the abbot had his own office, the abbot's kuti, the death room, Suchinno's work room, the dining hall and other buildings.

Away from this clutch of buildings, and in the rear of the complex, were about three dozen kutis scattered about on the grounds surrounding our monastery's bo tree, a large bodhi tree, the sort under which the Lord Buddha had sat when he had achieved enlightenment. Every monastery had its own bo tree, and it was especially cared for. Beneath our own there were a variety of Buddha images and statues, some of which had been there so long the tree roots had grown around them. It was a favorite place for many of the monks to sit and meditate. The temple dogs also enjoyed lounging there in the shade.

The more senior monks lived in the kutis that surrounded the bo tree. One didn't have to live in a kuti, but some monks preferred the solitude and quiet, hard to come by items for those living in the main dormitory.

Trees were abundant, but there was little grass to speak of. Concrete footpaths had been laid down, wandering here and there among the trees, connecting all the kutis and various bathrooms together and circling around the bo tree.

Most of the kutis had a kuti boy, chosen from the many "dek wats," or temple boys, that we cared for. The kuti boy went with the monk on his alms round, carrying the bag or bucket, which held the food that the community offered. The boys were responsible for keeping their respective kuti clean and swept, and serving as personal assistants for the monks they were assigned to, should the monk require it. In return, the monk saw to the needs of the boy, gave him instruction in the dharma, and very often served as a sort of substitute father, or elder brother.

My almost-kuti-boy Jak was an orphan and his left leg had been crippled thanks to a bout of childhood polio — when life hands out its bad news, some people have all the luck. He'd lost both parents to AIDS, his father many years ago, his mother, infected by her husband, only last year. An uncle had been glad to take him in — in exchange for back-breaking labor, day after day after endless day. After a few months of that, Jak stole enough money for bus fare from his uncle's wallet and left for Bangkok, eventually winding up at Wat Mahanat a few months ago in search of food, of which he'd not had enough for quite some time.

Jak went with me in the mornings on my alms round, and I often took him places and did as much "mentoring" as I could.

Only boys whom the abbot thought would benefit from such closeness to a monk were allowed to become kuti boys. These were usually the upcountry kids who had wandered into Bangkok, or orphans, or those who had not yet become corrupted by Bangkok and its ways. Most of these boys needed only the presence of an elder brother or father figure to help keep them on the straight and narrow.

I was now walking through the midst of the kutis on the concrete footpaths, lost in my own thoughts. We had a dead boy, and now a monk who had been missing since yesterday morning — the classic 1-2 punch, the victim, the perpetrator who flees the scene. If Banditto was indeed the killer, then what remained was to establish some link between him and the boy, or to supply some motive as to why he had killed him, something that we could write down on a report and be satisfied with and dismiss the matter from our minds.

Brother Banditto was one of the younger monks, and he had stayed in the main dormitory.

I crossed the grounds, wanting now to see his cell, to see if it might turn up any clues, either to his disappearance or the death of the boy.

His cell, as I discovered, was on the second floor of the main dormitory, room number 245. The door was closed.

I opened it and went inside, and found pretty much what I expected — and some things I did not. There was a thin mattress on the floor with a cotton blanket lying on it, and a small pillow. A Buddha statue on a small table sat in the corner of the room. An electric fan. A few books. A box with an extra set of robes in it, and some other clothes, like socks and underwear.

Monks were only supposed to do one of two things in their kuti or cell: They should either sleep, or meditate. The surroundings and furnishings were to reflect this, as was indeed the case here. What bothered me was the set of robes, neatly folded and lying to one side of his bed. The abbot only allowed monks to have two sets of robes, and if there was one in the box and another by his bed, then Banditto had "fled the scene" wearing nothing but a sarong, which I thought rather unlikely.

I knelt down next to his bed, feeling the blanket, picking up the pillow, looking under the mattress. Underneath the mattress was a small bag containing syringes, little wax packets filled with a powdery substance that I suspected was heroin, lighters, and a large spoon with burn marks on the bottom, which had undoubtedly been used to heat the heroin.

Was our Brother Banditto a heroin addict? Had he been giving heroin to Nong Noi? That would account for the needle marks I had seen on the boy's arms.

The taking of intoxicants was forbidden in the Five Precepts, upon which all of the rest of Buddhism was built — not to take life, not to lie, not to steal, not to engage in sexual misconduct, and not to indulge in intoxicants.

I went to the window and looked out, finding an excellent view of the parking lot. I tried to imagine Banditto leaving, dressed in a sarong, and found I could not. If it had been late at night, he would have had to scale the wall or the gates. If it had been at night, for that matter, then what had happened to make him flee? Even if he had killed Nong Noi, he would have had time to dress properly, and he would have made time, if he knew he had to flee. The only other explanation was that he had stolen clothes, perhaps from the youth program — if he was on the run, he would not want to be wearing monk's robes. And yet trying to disguise a shaved head and shaved eyebrows would require more than a stolen pair of jeans and a T-shirt.

If he had killed Nong Noi, I would have expected him to have done it in his cell, where he could close the door and hope for a bit of privacy. But there was nothing about the room to suggest that someone had been murdered in it — no dried blood on the floor, no knocked over furniture, nothing to suggest a struggle.

In fact, there wasn't much about this room to suggest that a person had actually lived here. Although monks are encouraged to give up attachments, especially to objects, we seem to collect "stuff" like everyone else. Much of it is donated to us by those wishing to make merit, which we accept and then try to give away if we don't really need it.

But there are still things that begin to pile up: Business cards, little pieces of paper with notes on them, Buddha images — medals or medallions, bus ticket stubs, dharma tapes, an extra pair of sandals, and whatnot, none of which I saw in his room.

Brother Banditto had either been a very holy man, or had collected all his things and fled the scene. The only other option would be that he kept most of his personal items somewhere else. Why would anyone want to do that? And where would one be able to keep such things?

I left the main dormitory, troubled.

Something else was tugging at me — something about the bathroom where the body had been discovered. Had I overlooked something this morning?

My footsteps took me back in that direction, and soon I was standing outside the door, looking in. I went in, and tried to picture in my mind what had happened here. There were two obvious choices. The boy had come into this bathroom alive, and had been killed inside it. Or he had been killed elsewhere, and carried here, his body dumped in the water jar.

If the boy had been burned with cigarettes, where were the cigarette butts? I had examined the floor and the grounds outside very closely, but there had been no signs of cigarette ash or butts.

I stepped up to the water jar and peered inside. The water was murky, but I could see through to the bottom. There was nothing inside the basin but water. Or was there? I bent closer, my nose almost touching the surface of the water, peering downwards.

There was something.

I folded my robes back around my shoulder, and stuck a hand down in the water, scooping up a small dark brown object.

It was a Buddhist medal, a medallion, the sort worn by many monks and the faithful.

Had the killer left it behind? Had the boy been wearing it? It did not have water stains on it, could not have been in the water all that long.

I put it in my pocket.

There were other questions. If the boy had been killed inside the bathroom, there should be blood somewhere, or feces or urine — victims often evacuate their bowels when they die. But the scene was too clean. That suggested the boy had been murdered elsewhere, and had been brought here. But where had the boy been killed? The bottoms of his feet had been far too clean for me to believe that he had walked to the bathroom of his own accord.

I went outside and walked slowly to the monastery wall, lost in my thoughts. It was like the beginnings of a jigsaw puzzle. A few tantalizing pieces. Possibilities. One had to get a sense of what the whole picture was first, before the pieces could start being fit together.

I walked slowly along the length of the wall, looking for any indentations in the dirt that would suggest footprints. There did not seem to be any.

Feeling a bit foolish, I hoisted myself up, orange robes and all, onto the monastery wall, to have a look on the other side, to see if anything had been thrown over it. The monastery wall was set against the edge of a soi, or alley, and there were numerous shop houses on the other side, with a line of cars moving down the soi, interspersed with motorcyclists.

I knew what it must look like for a monk to be climbing over a wall, but did not care, and I kept my eyes averted from those who were staring at me.

I jumped to the ground and began walking, searching through the bushes and plants along the wall. I went all the way down to the end, and then retraced my steps, but there was nothing to be found.

Embarrassed again, I climbed back over the wall.

It was obvious that Nong Noi had been murdered inside the monastery complex.

But where?

Ten

I saw Jak coming across the grounds, limping as he always did, wearing billowy shorts and a tank top.

"Paw!" he called, using the affectionate word for father.

I hated being called that.

"There's a phone call for you. Brother Kittisaro sent me to find you."

"Don't call me paw," I said, rather rudely.

He lowered his face and wouldn't look at me, sensing that he had somehow displeased me, as if his kindness had been thrown back in his face — as indeed it had been. Why had I done that? Why did I always do that when it came to this boy? It wasn't that I disliked him. Or was it?

I tried to tell myself that he needed to learn proper respect, that he should address me formally, that familiarity with a Buddhist monk was unbecoming. But I knew the truth of the matter was something else altogether.

Jak was a handsome thirteen-year-old boy. He had a round face that gave way to a large jaw with a brilliant set of teeth. There was a certain sort of impishness and good humor in his eyes. He was strong in all the right places, and had a gentle trusting disposition. He seemed incapable of harming anyone. If it wasn't for his leg, he might well have become one of those souls who manage to get through life on their good looks, charming their way into opportunities that seemed to fall into their laps from all sides. But his leg made him an outcast, someone to be pitied, stared at, whispered about, and looked down upon.

He was tall, all elbows and knees, lanky, caught in that awkward place between boyhood and manhood, full of insecurities, his body changing, hormones raging, wondering what his place was in this world, what life would hold for him, what he could hope for.

I glanced at him and felt bad about my harsh words. I wanted to apologize. But instead, I said, "The abbot might not like it if he heard you calling me that."

He wouldn't look at me, but he nodded.

The words "I'm sorry" were right there on my tongue, almost demanding to be said, but I remained silent. The boy had so little reason to be happy. Why did I begrudge him any little display of affection?

We went to the main office. Whoever had called was still waiting, and Kittisaro handed me the phone, a strange look on his face.

"Hello?"

"Is that you, Brother Ananda? I saw the paper this morning. One of my boys has been killed. I'd like a progress report. Abbot said you were in charge."

"Really," I said, a bit bewildered. "May I ask who's calling?"

"Certainly." The voice was confident, aggressive, the sort that was used to issuing orders and being obeyed. "Police Major General Chao, at police general headquarters."

"Are you related to the victim, sir?" I asked, trying to make the connection.

"Not exactly, Ananda. I'm the one who funds the youth program there. I fund it personally, for that matter, with my own money. That's why I say they're *my* boys. Now, I wonder if you could tell me what happened. I'm not funding your program so my boys can get murdered, am I?"

I took a breath, shook my head, completely thrown. I was not aware that our youth program was funded by anyone besides the monastery itself, least not anyone who considered the boys as somehow being his own. And a major general ... that was a bit high up the ladder, and I was not pleased that such a person would be breathing down my neck wanting progress reports.

I tried to give a brief summary of what had happened, what we had discovered, but there wasn't much to say.

"And you say one of the monks is missing?" he asked.

"Yes, one of them is."

"That monk have a name, by any chance?"

"Yes, he did. Brother Banditto."

"Banditto?"

"Yes."

"Banditto?" he repeated again, as if he didn't believe me.

"Yes," I said, rather impatiently.

"Hmmm. Well, thanks for your time, brother. I'll be in touch."

Chao rang off before I could so much as say good-bye.

How odd.

Jak touched me on the arm.

"Do you want me to do anything else for you, Father Ananda?" he asked, face still full of hurt.

His hair was hanging in his eyes — just the way my son's once had. My heart went out to him. I wanted nothing but good things to happen to him, although I knew there would be more bad than good — in a society where family is valued above all else, to not have one is to exist in some in-between state that was, I suspected, worse than death itself. And in a society where sameness was valued, to be different — to have a crippled limb — was to be singled out, to be mocked, to be rejected, looked upon with pitying eyes, with nothing much ever expected of you. Partly this had to do with karma, with the belief that the crippled and fatherless and poverty stricken were being punished for sins in a past life. It was their own fault. If that was true, then what had happened to me was also my own fault, and I wasn't sure I would ever be able to bring myself to believe that.

"Reverend Father Ananda?"

That stiffly formal title sounded strange on his lips. It lacked the affection and spontaneity of *paw*. Was that what I had wanted? Was I happy now that I had reduced this boy to addressing me by my proper title?

I closed my eyes, put a hand to my forehead.

"No, I don't need anything," I said.

I tried not to notice the hurt look on his face, the dejection that sank into his shoulders.

I left the main office to find a secluded, quiet place where I could sit down and be alone with my thoughts.

Eleven

I signed out at the main office, telling Kittisaro I needed to check out something and would be back in a couple of hours. With the address for "Jut and her husband" in my hand, I walked through the main gates to our monastery and boarded a bus which took me into the heart of Chinatown.

Shop houses were piled on top of shop houses. Small businesses flourished everywhere. Vendors pushed carts, laid their wares out on the street. A visit to Chinatown was like stepping into another world. Traffic was particularly dense, and I had to pick my way through snaking lines of it to find the address written on the piece of paper. I eventually found myself staring a shop house that housed a small restaurant on the ground floor, selling duck dishes, manned by a haggard woman who was simultaneously watching over three small children.

"I'm looking for a woman named Jut," I said to her, when she had settled her latest batch of customers at an old, metal table, with plastic footstools for seats.

"What do you want?" she asked rather unkindly. "If it's about Noi, don't bother. I'm not bailing him out of anything else. I'm sick of that boy and his problems."

She wouldn't give me her eyes. She had the sort of demeanor that suggested disaster could fall down from the sky at any moment, and that she had dodged so many blows she could no longer keep up.

"It's rather more complicated than bailing him out," I said quietly.

She stopped what she was doing — chopping meat on a large chopping block — and looked at me with haggard eyes. "Who are you?"

I explained who I was. "Nong Noi has been killed," I said. "I found your address among his possessions. I'm wondering if you were related."

She took the butcher knife and sank it into the cutting board with an angry flick of her wrist. "He's my cousin," she said, turning away to wash her hands. I waited patiently for her to finish, and I saw her shoulders shaking and suspected she was crying. When she turned back to me, she seemed more composed. "Could I offer you some water, something to drink?"

I accepted gratefully, and she fetched a cold glass of water.

"What happened?" she asked.

"That's what I'm trying to figure out. It appears that he's been murdered. Aside from that, there isn't much I can say. His body was discovered early this morning. Has he been to see you lately?"

She shook her head. "My husband doesn't like him. Doesn't want him around the kids. I can't say I blame him."

"Why is that?"

"Well, he's a drug addict, isn't he?" she said. "I let him stay with us once and found him shooting up on our sofa. My husband was furious. I told him he had to go. But he was always like that, always getting himself into trouble, wouldn't abide by anybody's rules. He was always such a pain in the ass, and pardon me for saying it."

"When was the last time you saw him?" I asked.

She looked around her small shop, satisfying herself that her customers weren't being inconvenienced by our conversation. "Couple of months ago, I guess. He was hungry. I fed him but told him he had to leave before my husband came home. He came by in the late afternoon."

"How are you related?"

"His mother was my mother's sister," she said.

"Was?"

She nodded. "My aunt hanged herself, last year, from what I heard. I guess she couldn't stand it anymore. I don't know. I always felt sorry for her and those kids."

"She committed suicide?"

Jut nodded. "Those kids scattered. Noi came to Bangkok, wanted to stay with us, but he was such a mess, we just couldn't let him. He'd leave his syringes around and the kids would find them and play with them — I mean, what were we supposed to do? He wouldn't work, wouldn't get a job, didn't seem like he wanted to help himself. All he wanted was those drugs. You just couldn't keep him away from them. And all he ever did was cause problems."

I listened to this in silence. She excused herself to tend to her customers. When she returned, I asked, "Do you know anyone who might have wanted to kill him?"

She laughed, but it had a rather bitter sound to it.

"Sure. Just about everybody who knew him."

Twelve

The afternoon tea of fruit juices had assuaged my hunger somewhat, but now, with the evening chanting about to get underway, I was famished.

I sat cross-legged with the senior monks, waiting for the abbot to arrive. The younger monks sat behind the senior monks in the prayer hall. The temple boys could be heard outside playing a game of football. The sun had fallen and darkness was about to descend.

My stomach rumbled rather loudly, and Father Thammarato, sitting to my immediate right in his customary spot, turned to glance at me, offering a knowing smile.

I was distracted from my thoughts by the arrival of the abbot, who proceeded up to the front and sat himself down ceremonially, surrounded by his attendants.

"Before we begin, brothers," the abbot said quietly, "I should like to inform you that one of our boys was found dead this morning on the monastery grounds. No doubt you have heard of it by now. I should like to inform you that Father Ananda is looking into the matter, and requires your full co-operation, should he call upon you for any reason."

Several pairs of eyes sought me out, and I lowered my own in embarrassment.

Father Thammarato elbowed me in the ribs playfully, as if it was a great game indeed.

"Let us remember Nong Noi," the abbot continued. "Let us hope his next life will be more fortunate than this one. And it goes without saying that if you know anything about what happened to him, please inform Father Ananda accordingly. Starting tomorrow, we will offer the three days of funeral chants for Nong Noi before he is cremated. I expect all of you to be in attendance on all three days, and I will accept no excuses for absence unless you have a prior obligation. While it's indeed true that mourners often pay you to chant at their funeral rites, this is one case where I hope your compassion for our boys will persuade you to forgo such payment and offer honest prayers on behalf of the deceased. I hope I have made myself perfectly clear."

The abbot had, I knew. He had gently rebuked the greedier monks who refused to offer funeral chants unless they were paid — as if they were businessmen!

The abbot went silent then, casting his eyes down, his ceremonial fan on his lap. Then, in a ritual that was ages-old, he gripped the fan by its long wooden handle and planted the point firmly on the ground in front of him, the fan part blocking the sight of his face.

I had my own fan, as we each did, and we all followed suit.

And then the abbot began the chant, and I lost myself in the flowing, sonorous Pali words that continued on, without stopping, for the next forty-five minutes.

And all the while, I saw Nong Noi's sightless eyes staring back at me with a question I could not yet answer:

Who killed me?

CHAPTER TWO

" 'He abused me, he beat me, he defeated me, he robbed me': the hatred of those who harbor such thoughts is not appeased."

The Lord Buddha. From the Dhammapada, #3.

One

The monastery's gong rang at four in the morning on the next day, and I woke with a start. The temple dogs began howling and barking right away, as if they had waited all night for the chance to have at it. Another day had begun.

I got to my feet slowly, various bones and joints popping and cracking. I tightened the sarong around my waist and wiped at my eyes, paid my morning homage to the Buddha, went out on the porch, and immediately began thinking about Nong Noi. But I was a monk, not a police officer, and the problem of. Nong Noi would have to wait.

In the large communal bath, I splashed cold water over my shoulders and shaved head and rejoiced in the feel of it. Other monks did likewise, a long row of them, standing before large earthen jars, ladling water with plastic bowls. They each wore a sarong, which got wet in the process, but modesty would not permit otherwise.

I let my eyes wander. I loved these men, even the cranky, unbalanced ones, of which there were more than a few. They were my family. There were times when I was certain I would never leave them, never again ask more from life than what I already had. There were times when I could see myself living out my days among them, as one of them, truly one of them, my heart no longer divided.

But there were other times when I wasn't so sure.

I thought of women, as most of the monks do. I went through phases of remembering what it was like to be in my wife's arms, when we had made love, when we had whispered words that only lovers could bring themselves to say. Such phases tormented me, stirring up lust and desire. At times, I wanted nothing more than to give up the robes and lay down with the first woman who would have me. My mind offered up endless fantasies about what it would be like, how it would feel, the curves, the softness, the pleasure.

Reality, I know, was likely to be much different.

Outside, the morning air was cool on my bare skin, and I walked back quickly to my kuti. Inside, I began the somewhat difficult process of putting on my monk's robes. They were basically sheets, and it required a fair bit of doing to get them all properly wound and wrapped and in place. Dressing had been a nightmare during my first few months as a monk, and I was never certain as to when exactly my robes would slide off, exposing my nakedness to the laughter and amusement of others. But by now I had gotten the hang of it, and it was my turn to watch the younger monks expose themselves, and I must confess to laughing right along with everyone else.

The morning chant was soon over, and I lined up with the other monks, preparing to leave the monastery and go on the alms round. Jak was dressed in his usual shorts and tank top, and he offered me a shy smile as came to stand by my side, ready to accompany me, already carrying the yellow bucket we would use to collect the offerings. He didn't use his smile very often, but he always made an exception for me. It was another thing for which I felt immensely guilty — I didn't often give him any reason to smile, despite his kindness to me.

The oldest monks went first, followed by the younger ones. I was among the first to walk out the monastery gates and into the quiet city streets. As we did every morning, we split up, each of the monks going on their own route, none of which overlapped that of another.

The morning alms round wasn't a begging excursion. Monks were not allowed to beg for anything. On the contrary, what we were doing was presenting ourselves to the lay people and providing them with the opportunity to earn merit by offering us food and the necessities of life. If no one wished to avail themselves of the opportunity, we returned empty-handed and that was that. And although there were times when that had probably happened, it was more common to find all sorts of people standing in front of their homes, waiting for the opportunity to offer food.

With Jak following behind respectfully and quietly, with his strange limp that everyone stared at and pitied (and which hadn't done a thing for his self-esteem), I walked slowly down the main thoroughfare — Rama IV — keeping my eyes cast down, striving to remain mindful and aware. On our alms rounds, we were to keep in mind the four things that every monk needs: Food, clothing, medicine, shelter. We were also to conduct ourselves in a way that would not bring disgrace or discredit to the monkhood, thus we kept our eyes down, walked barefooted and appropriately robed, and spoke quietly, if at all.

We walked the usual three blocks down and then turned into a side street where we began to collect offerings from the Buddhist faithful. The street was lined with people, mostly older women with their daughters, who stood waiting to offer us something.

I went to the first of these, not speaking. The woman standing there, as she had done every day for years, offered a wai of respect and asked if she might be able to offer me something. Since monks may not touch women, I carried a cloth, and allowed her to put her food on the cloth. I then held the cloth for Jak so that he could collect it and put it into my alms bowl. I offered the standard, brief chant of blessing.

We moved on to the next person, and the process repeated itself. Down the street, everywhere we went, lay Buddhists were standing and waiting, ready to offer food, sweets, and toothpaste, even money. Each placed the offering on my cloth. Jak removed the offering and put it in the alms bowl, and eventually the bucket, which became increasingly heavy. Even motorcycles zoomed to a halt beside us, the driver making an offering and then speeding away. Some of the people asked for special blessings, and knelt down in the street while I offered them.

In all, it took more than an hour. Afterward, we made our way back to the monastery, walking slowly, dodging the stray dogs, trying to avoid the garbage left on the streets, walking past pot holes large enough to ground army tanks.

We collected far more food than one person could eat in a given day, but that wasn't strictly the point. The food we collected also went to the boys that the monastery housed, as well as elderly or sick monks who could not make the rounds, and anyone else who happened to be around at meal time and was hungry.

With the other senior monks, I sat in a circle on the floor. The novice monks sat in their own circle, at some distance away, to signify that they were not yet fully ordained. We ate in silence.

When I had finished, I fetched Jak.

"Maybe you could help me today," I said quietly.

"Sure," he said, beaming, as if all my previous unkindnesses were already forgiven and forgotten, at least as far as he was concerned.

We walked through the monastery grounds, slowly, without hurrying. He was very self-conscious of the way he walked, and always stayed just behind me, as if he didn't want me to see him.

"What happened to Nong Noi, Father Ananda? I mean, what really happened?"

"That's what we're going to figure out," I said.

"You mean 'you,' don't you?"

"No," I said kindly, giving him a sideways glance. "I meant 'us.' I want you to help me figure out what happened."

The excitement in the boy's eyes was impossible to miss. "Really?" he exclaimed. "You're not just having me on?"

"Really," I said. "But keep it to yourself, alright?"

The boy nodded. "He was murdered, wasn't he? That's what everyone is saying. And Banditto's missing, and everyone's saying he did it. Had to."

I didn't reply.

Our footsteps took us in the direction of my kuti, where I retrieved my monk's bag, and put on my "city shoes" — plastic flip-flops were fine for messing about the monastery, but the city streets required something a bit more substantial.

"Are we going out?" the boy asked excitedly.

"We certainly are," I said.

As a monk, I could not handle money myself, so I instructed the youth to go see the temple treasurer and ask for bus fare and lunch money for the two of us. Jak happily agreed and went off, and I watched — I confess — as his hips went up and down in that strange gait, one leg shorter than the other, one leg strong with muscle and over-developed, the other weak. Sometimes I felt that he and I were much the same, one too strong, the other too weak, and yet together we could function, together we somehow made a complete person. We were both wounded in our own ways.

Jak returned with a 500-baht note, eager to set off.

On our way out, I caught sight of Mrs. Nuan, the fruit-seller who always set up shop by the gates leading to the main road. I greeted her and she returned my greeting with a wide smile. She was a large, no-nonsense woman, and always wore an old-style farmer's hat, the sort made of bamboo that looked somewhat like a lampshade. If I had to stand in the sun all day selling fruit, I supposed such a hat wouldn't be all that bad.

I wanted to talk to her because she knew all the goings-on at Wat Mahanat, and in the past had always been a useful source of information. "Mrs. Nuan," I said, pausing, not looking at her, for I was forbidden to do that (although the sight of a sixty-seven-year-old woman wearing a lampshade probably wouldn't rouse much desire in my loins, but that wasn't strictly the point).

"Yes, Reverend Father?"

I wasn't a "reverend father" — an abbot — but she called all the monks by that title, as did many other people. Titles were a bit difficult anyway. They depended on who was being addressed, and one's relationship to that person. Only the abbot was a "reverend father." Elder monks were properly called "Father" by those lower in seniority. Younger monks and novices, when addressed by elder monks, were called "Brother" or "Younger Brother" or even "Little Brother." Thus it was proper for my kuti boy Jak to address me as "Father Ananda" while I addressed Kittisaro as "Brother Kittisaro," although both Kittisaro and I had been in the robes for the same amount of time and we were both technically "fathers."

Another common form of address was to call a monk "Bhikku," the Pali word for "monk." So sometimes I was addressed as "Ananda Bhikku,"or "Monk Ananda." Among familiars, the titles were often dropped altogether, and I was just "Ananda," but this happened only among close associates of approximately the same age and rank.

It got even more confusing when dealing with monks who had royal titles and were making their way up the Buddhist hierarchy.

To be safe, then, many chose the term "Reverend Father," perhaps wanting to error on the side of caution.

"You've heard about our unfortunate discovery," I said quietly to Mrs. Nuan.

"Oh, indeed I have," she replied. "And such a sweet boy he was."

"Did you know him?" I asked, knowing that she very likely did — there wasn't much about our goings-on that escaped her ever-watchful eyes, and the boys often pestered her. And you never knew what you might turn up when you went around interviewing people, even those who didn't seem to have any connection to the crime in question.

"Of course," she replied straight off. "Know all the boys, I do — they're forever begging watermelon or pineapple from me, and I haven't the heart to tell them no. Course I know perfectly well some of the boys have money in their pockets — Nong Noi certainly did — but I would never ask them to pay. Figure it's my way of making merit, doing a good deed, all that."

"Money in his pocket?" I repeated, curious.

"Well, yes," she replied. "New sneakers, nice clothes. I mean, it was obvious, wasn't it?"

And then she would say no more.

"Obvious?" I prompted.

"Well, you know," she said.

"I'm afraid I don't," I said kindly.

"Well, I don't want to gossip, Reverend Father."

"And you wouldn't be," I said. "I'm trying to figure out what happened to Nong Noi, so if you know something that would be relevant or important, please feel free to tell me. Gossip is another matter altogether, Mrs. Nuan."

This freed her tongue.

"Well," she said conspiratorially, "there have been rumors, people talking, wondering ... some of those boys, father, well,

I don't know where they get those clothes, but I have my suspicions. All these motorcycles coming and going. You know."

I waited, but she would say no more.

"What about the motorcycles?"

"Well, they're selling something, aren't they? Making deliveries? I have to ask myself, delivering what? To whom? What sort of business is it? But they're awfully secretive, those boys, so I don't really know for certain. But there are some as say it must be drugs, Reverend Father. And the way some of those boys look — glassy-eyed, laughing all the time, or stumbling around — why, one of them came in on his bike and damn near knocked my cart over, if you'll pardon my language. Made me right angry, he did. But surely you know all this?"

I shook my head. I most certainly did not. In fact, I avoided going to the front of the compound if I possibly could because of the noise of the motorcycles and the youths hanging around and the general busy-ness of it all. If there was any enemy to my mindfulness and concentration, that was it.

"You've been very helpful, Mrs. Nuan," I said.

"I hope you figure out what happened to that poor boy," she said. "And let's hope it doesn't happen to any of the others."

Indeed.

Jak, during this conversation, had been standing right behind me, like a shadow.

"Let's be off, then," I said.

"Where're we going?" he inquired.

"I should like to speak to a reporter who may have been the last person to see Nong Noi alive — except, of course, for the one who killed him."

Two

The offices to Thai Rath were a bit messier than I had expected. The posh reception area soon gave way to less-than-posh working areas. Stacks of papers were everywhere: Piled in corners, on desks, on stairs. Dozens of reporters sat at desks, typing away furiously in front of computers, or congregating around television sets or water coolers.

"If you'll just wait here a moment," the receptionist said, indicating a long couch in the foyer outside the editorial department. "I'll see if Jentara is available."

I sat down, but Jak remained standing, too excited for his own good.

"Thai Rath," he said in admiration. "I wonder if we'll get to see someone famous."

I was more concerned about whether I would be able to see the reporter who had given Nong Noi her business card — and whether she would speak to me about what transpired during their conversation, or not.

We waited a full ten minutes before the receptionist returned, followed by a short, dumpy woman with close-cut hair, wearing men's clothing.

"Sorry to keep you waiting, reverend father," the receptionist said. "This is Jentara. If you'll excuse me?"

The receptionist left us to make our own introductions.

"I need to talk to you about something," I said. "Is this a good time?"

The woman shrugged. "Will it take long? I've got a deadline. A story. I need to finish it."

"Won't take long at all," I said gently. "By the way, this is my assistant Jak. Jak, say hello to Ms. Jentara."

Jak managed to mumble some sort of greeting, and the reporter merely smiled, masking her irritation.

I produced the envelope with the reporter's business card. "Is this yours, by any chance?" I asked, showing it to her but not allowing her to touch it.

She nodded. "Where did you find it?"

I offered an embarrassed smile. "On a dead body, and pardon my bluntness. A boy named Nong Noi who was living at my temple — Wat Mahanat. Have you heard of it?"

"Of course," the woman said.

"Do you remember this boy? He was about seventeen."

"Of course," she said again, but offering no more than that.

"Would it be impolite of me to inquire about your conversation?"

"Of course it would be, Reverend Father."

I smiled, hoping to smooth over any potentially embarrassing confrontation. "And even so, I should like to inquire. I used to be a police officer, and I've been called upon me to investigate the death of this young boy. He was found in a bathroom. His manner of death was rather brutal. I found your card among his personal effects. I was thinking there might be a connection."

"You mean, you think I killed him?" the woman asked, outraged.

"No, of course not," I said quickly. "I mean, if he had gone to see you, he must have had a reason. I have to ask myself, why would a young boy go see a reporter at a newspaper like this? Did he know you? Were you related? If not, then he must have had some story to tell. Did that story have anything to do with his murder? That sort of thing. But goodness no, I don't think you had anything to do with his death."

This seemed to give her pause for thought. She did not seem unkind, but rather tough, hard as nails, as a woman, I thought, would have to be in the sort of profession she was in.

"He told me some story about drugs at the temple — wheeling and dealing and all of that. I told him I needed proof, evidence, that I couldn't just print anything, that it had to be backed up with facts. I told him to bring me some evidence, some facts, and then I would think about it."

"Think about what?" I asked.

"An expose," she said, gazing at me and not taking her eyes away.

"I see," I said, and it was my turn to be quiet. An expose. Of my temple. Alas, monks and scandals went hand in hand and it seemed like every week another story was printed about some temple somewhere engaged in unholy business. But I had always thought of it as other temples, as the problem of other monks. What would such a story do to my own temple, to my own abbot, to the monks I deemed friends and family?

It would be devastating.

"I see," I said again. "If there is wrong-doing going on at the temple, of course you are quite right to report it."

"So you think this boy's story was legit?" she asked, coming to life — she could smell a story, or at least the makings of one.

"I don't know," I said honestly. "All I know is that he got himself killed, so something must be going on."

"Would you care to speculate?"

"No, I would not," I said. "I'd like to know if there was anything the boy told you that might help me figure out who killed him."

"And if I help you, what are you going to do for me?"

She crossed her arms over her chest and waited.

I smiled. "We can make a deal, then," I said. "You help me, I'll help you. But by the book. No stories until we know what we're dealing with. But when there's something to write about, you'll be the first to know."

"Okay," she said, fetching a small notebook from her back pants pocket, and grabbing a pen that was lodged behind an ear. "How about your real name, for starters?" She put pen to paper. "Since you already know mine."

My real name. I thought about that, and couldn't resist grinning. I had a real name, of course, the name I was born with, and had used for close to 40 years. But I had left that name — and that person — behind when I had joined the monastery.

"I have given you my real name," I said. "Father Ananda. Wat Mahanat. Rama IV Road. If you have any inquiries about me, you can direct them there, and I'll leave it to the abbot to decide whether giving out my real name is important or not."

"Fine," she said, "so you're not an impostor monk looking for your fifteen minutes then?"

"I should think not," I said.

"Fine. So what's going on?"

I had to admire her spunk, but I had come to interview her, and not the other way around.

"How about you telling me about your conversation with Nong Noi?"

"What's to tell," she said, shrugging. "Same old, same old, heard it a thousand times if I've heard it once. Monks engaged in dirty business — gambling, bootlegging, drugs, 'insert your favorite vice here.' If not engaged in such activities, then profiting from them — money laundering, hiding wanted criminals behind the orange robes, sheltering them, hiding their money for them, for a share, of course. Noi's story was just more of the same. I told him I needed facts, figures, papers, bank statements, pictures, something, anything, the usual stuff. Can't just print anything, can we? And most of those stories are bogus anyway. Things get taken out of context, or someone has a score to settle, or wants revenge, and so makes something up — that sort of thing. And we've been burned on this type of story before. We print something and find out it's not really the truth, not really an accurate reflection of what was going on. So we have to be careful. And anyway, I've been assigned this beat now, so I don't do anything without proof, without evidence. I'm not about to let some stranger come in off the street and offer a wild tale without checking the facts and making sure there's a real story there before we print it. I mean, I've got a reputation to think about."

I cast my eyes to the floor, embarrassed. Monks have been taking a beating at the hands of reporters like this, and in some ways, we deserve every bit of it. But there's more to the story than just the scandals and poor judgments of a handful of monks who have brought disgrace upon us all. My own experience had been proof enough that the average monk is a sincere seeker after truth and enlightenment, honestly struggling to put the Lord Buddha's teachings into practice, which is not at all an easy thing to do. We weren't all greedy fiends. Yet for a reporter, that's not nearly as interesting as a monk caught with his pants down (or his robes around his ankles) or with his hands in a cookie jar or on a porno magazine.

Still, she was trying to be fair, and I gave her credit for that.

"Did he mention any names?" I asked.

"Not that I remember. He said there was a homeless shelter at the temple, and that some of the monks were getting some of the boys involved with drugs, having them make deliveries in return for shooting up, something to that effect. He said he looked in one of the packages he was supposed to deliver and found it was full of tablets in wax paper, very suspicious looking. He said he was trying to get out of it, but they wouldn't let him, and they tied him to a chair and burned him with cigarettes once, telling him they were going to do a lot worse things if he ever caused trouble. He was scared to death. He showed me those burns too, so at least that part of the story was true."

"But the rest of it wasn't?"

"Reverend Father, we get a lot of people coming in here telling us a lot of stories. They don't always pan out. I mean, they sound real convincing, but you start digging into them, and you find it's all hogwash. People want to get their names in the paper, and they think they can come in and just tell us anything and we'll write a story about it. Doesn't work that way."

"But you did see those cigarette burns?"

"I certainly did," she said. "They were still red and puffy — he said they had done it the day before. I guess he thought if he could get a story printed, they would be arrested or something, and his problems would be over."

"He didn't mention any names, any at all?"

She thought for a while but then slowly shook her head. "I mean, I wasn't very nice to him. He seemed to be a bit flaky, if you know what I mean."

I knew what she meant.

"So what can you tell me?" she asked.

What, indeed?

THREE

We stood outside the offices to Thai Rath, and I looked up and down a street choked with vehicles of all descriptions and sizes. There were cars, of course, so many that it was hard to believe we were in the midst of a bitter economic meltdown that began in 1997 with the collapse of the currency. One would expect to see fewer BMWs on the streets, but just the opposite was true. There were also huge lorries and swarms of motorcyclists, not known for obeying traffic rules, not even known for driving on the correct side of the street — not even sidewalks were sacred when it came to motorcyclists and their need to get where they were going as quickly as possible and pedestrians could just get out of the way, thank you.

Mixed in with this mess were tuk-tuks — little three-wheel vehicles with open-air back seats — and buses, bicyclists, homeless dogs, and more petrol fumes and black clouds of exhaust fumes than anyone should ever have to breathe in, not to mention hordes of pedestrians and vendors either pushing or manning their carts, and the odd cat or two.

It was through this chaos that Jak and I walked, looking for a bus stop. Next on the agenda was to see Lt. Somchai, if we could. So, along with about hundred other people, we waited at a bus stop.

Bus after bus came hurtling into the stop, jamming on the brakes and slowing the bus down just enough that passengers could jump off while others jumped on, before the bus sped off to the next stop as if the drivers were preparing for the Indianapolis 500 and the passengers were no more than annoying inconveniences. Most of these city buses were belching long black clouds of smoke in our faces — Jak had brought a handkerchief to cover his nose, but I had forgotten, so I used the sleeve of my orange robes instead.

At last the bus we were waiting for roared into the bus stop, and we boarded, squeezing ourselves into the midst of a packed vehicle.

I hated riding buses. My powers of detachment weren't developed enough to endure it without getting exceedingly riled up.

For one thing, bus drivers and conductors generally despise monks because we are granted the privilege of free bus fares — they consider us "Yellow Tigers," or freeloaders. Very often, while boarding a bus, I could hear whispers of "Yellow Tiger coming" as the passengers moved out of the way to let me pass.

The situation was made worse because of the "monk's seat" which each bus has, and which monks are expected to sit in. It was always the seat right next to the door, so you could get a good lung-full of exhaust fumes each time the door was opened — whether that was intentional or not, I wouldn't venture to guess.

When I board a bus, if there is someone sitting there, they will jump up guiltily and take to standing while I'm well-nigh hustled into the seat as if I had no right to stand.

All of this was done out of respect for monks, of course, and I put up with it, knowing that some around me resented this small privilege and resented the fact that I didn't have to pay a bus fare either. If I thought about these things too much, I would wind up taking a taxi or simply walking.

The same ritual and fuss and smoldering resentment was about to occur. Jak was a willing participant, pushing me, with his body, in the direction of the monk's seat, which has just been vacated by a woman holding a baby in her arms.

I was going to have one of those moments when I needed to buck the tide and do things my way.

"You go ahead," I said to the woman with the baby. "It's alright."

She was trying to hold on to a strap overhead with one hand, the other cradling her baby over her shoulder, as the bus shot away from the stop and roared back into traffic and we all swayed on our feet, trying to maintain our balance. She made no move to reclaim her seat, keeping her face turned away from me, embarrassed that a monk was speaking to her in public, no doubt hating my guts for making her stand up and lose her seat.

Jak was pushing me again, trying to get me to take the seat.

"Let this woman sit down," I said patiently. "I can stand."

The eyes staring back at me were filled with disbelief. The ritual wasn't played this way. The monk was supposed to take the seat and be grateful, and not issue orders about what he did or did not want to do.

"Really," I said again, looking around to the passengers crammed cheek to jowl around me, "Let the woman sit. She has a baby. I'm perfectly capable of standing up. I don't want to sit down."

There was whispered murmuring over this, and eyes stared at me as if I was high on *yaa baa,* or maybe heroin. Sometimes I couldn't win for losing.

Jak pushed me again, and I turned around, annoyed. "Stop pushing me," I snapped. He looked hurt — he was only playing his role in this ritual, after all, only unthinkingly doing what he had been told to do.

The folks around me were getting antsy. They wanted me in the seat. Even though they resented me for it, they wanted me sitting in that seat, because that was how things were done. I knew if I stood my ground long enough, one of the healthy-looking young fellows with dyed hair and expensive clothes sitting comfortably nearby might possibly let his conscience get the best of him and stand up, offering the woman his seat.

One eventually did.

The woman sat down gratefully.

I sat down too, and Jak sat next to me since no one else wanted to, and the tension in the bus evaporated. We were all playing our roles properly again, and everyone was happily resenting me for my small privileges.

"Everyone was looking at you," Jak said in a whisper, bending close to my ear.

I shrugged.

"Well, really," he said.

"Really, what?" I asked.

He didn't know, of course.

"Look," I said, "you don't have to do what people expect you to do, or what they want you to do. You have to do what's right. Is it right for me to sit while a woman with a child has to stand?"

"But you're a monk," he said, as if that settled it.

"And I'm not carrying a baby, am I?" I replied.

He was no more concerned about young women with babies than anyone else on this bus, and that bothered me. Sometimes I wanted to take this boy and shake him hard enough that his self-preoccupation would dislodge itself, if only for a minute or two, if only to show that it was a possibility and I wasn't completely wasting my time. But then I remembered how self-preoccupied I was at that age, and what could I do but look the other way and sigh.

Four

We got off and made our way to the Silom Police Station, which looked much like every other police station in the city, including the one where I had once used to work. There was the same dingy white color, dirty steps, faded posters taped to faded walls, all sorts of benches with all sorts of people sitting on them or waiting around.

We walked up the steps, and I made my way to the wired-off receptionist, where I asked if Lt. Somchai was available. Because I was a monk, I was given preferential treatment, ushered into the inner sanctum and offered a chair to sit down in. I motioned for Jak to sit down while I remained standing. I was tired of sitting down.

For twenty minutes or more I remained standing, knowing that Lt. Somchai had been called over the radio, and was probably making his way back to the station on his motorcycle, probably struggling with the traffic chaos like everyone else.

Jak acquitted himself well. For about five minutes. Then he could sit no longer, and began pacing back and forth in front of the police station's trophy cabinet, trying to make out the names on the plaques.

A door then opened, and Lt. Somchai strode in. We exchanged greetings.

"I've brought a friend," I said, motioning for Jak to come and present himself, which he did, albeit rather ungracefully and shyly, as if being introduced to someone might possibly kill him. He had so little confidence in himself that I felt embarrassed for him. He seemed to think the only thing people noticed about him was the way he walked, and while of course they did notice just that, they also noticed that he was a rather handsome boy and had a wonderful smile — if he would just use it once in a while.

"Got a couple things I was hoping you would have a look at," I said.

He offered a polite smile. "Of course."

He led me toward his desk, situated in the midst of a sea of other desks. I followed. Jak did too, but I told him to wait.

"But I thought you said we were working together!" he exclaimed in a low, hurt voice.

"We are," I said. "But I need to speak privately with this man."

I received a rolled set of eyes and a long sigh. Dejection sank into his shoulders. He lowered them, lowered his eyes.

I reminded myself that patience was a virtue.

I took the chair opposite Somchai's desk. He handed me some photographs — the footprints in the bathroom. I produced the only bits of evidence I had: The business card for the reporter at Thai Rath, some of the newspaper from the black bag, and the small medallion I had found in the water jar.

"Can you do anything with these?" I asked. Options were limited, of course.

"We can check the card and the paper for fingerprints," he said, pushing them aside and picking up the medallion. "This will be more useful, I suspect."

I told him that I had found it in the water jar.

"Meaning that it probably belonged to the killer or the victim?" he asked.

I nodded.

"Do you know anything about this business of monks and medals?" he asked, chuckling.

I shook my head. I was not a very superstitious person and frankly couldn't bring myself to believe that wearing a medal made by Monk So and So would protect me from fire, or snake bite, or ensure that I had a baby boy, or any other such nonsense. But Buddhist medals were big business, and a distressing number of otherwise sane monks made a distressing amount of money designing and selling them.

"My wife's big on these things," Somchai said. "She's got so many magazines about them, I don't know what to do with them all. I keep threatening to throw them all away and she says she'll take a pair of scissors to my privates while I'm sleeping, if I do, so there you are. You want me to track this down?"

"If you can find out which temple it was made at, that would be wonderful."

"I'll see what I can do," he said. "You having any luck?"

I offered a small laugh. "I have some clues, some leads. I've got a missing monk now, speculation that he might have been the murderer, might have fled the scene, although I'm not so sure about that. We'll see where it goes."

"That would clear it all up, though, wouldn't it?" he asked.

It would. If Banditto could be found. Trouble was, he was not likely to be found, and there would always be a question hanging over Nong Noi's death.

"I have a favor to ask before I leave," I said. "My young friend out there, Jak, desperately needs to feel important. You know how kids are. He's had a rough life, doesn't think anything will ever get better, convinced the world hates him, and all of that, most of which is no doubt true. I was wondering if you'd give him your business card, tell him to call you if he ever gets in trouble and needs some help. It would give him a sense of security, make him feel like he's made a friend. It would mean a lot to him."

"That's not such a big favor. I'd be happy to do it. We have a youth league for football — did you know that? Why don't you tell him — well, I'll tell him — to come around on Saturday mornings for practice. We've got jerseys for the kids and everything. He'll love it."

We went back out to the reception area, and I excused myself and went to the restroom, and by the time I returned, Jak had a grin on his face that wouldn't quit.

Five

We took another bus and got off two stops before the monastery. While out and about, there was one more thing to do. Jak had been complaining about his empty stomach, and my own wasn't so hot either.

I was working on my attachments, or, I should say, on learning how not to be attached. But giving up Mrs. Buboi's noodles was simply not part of the game plan. Perhaps someday when I was close to perfect enlightenment, no longer ensnared by sense pleasures and desires, tottering on the edge of Nirvana with all my cravings perfectly extinguished, I would be able to turn my nose up when I passed Mrs. Buboi's noodle stand, but that would probably not be for a long time. And it certainly wouldn't be today because I'd been thinking about those noodles all morning and had the perfect excuse to stop by and eat them without feeling guilty.

"Reverend Father!" Mrs. Buboi exclaimed when we arrived during the noon rush. "Please, please, come, sit in the back."

She ushered us to the back of her small restaurant, where Jak and I seated ourselves at a private table she reserved for her own use, or that of her family and friends. Mrs. Buboi knew all about me and my lust for her noodles, and we had enacted this ritual numerous times before.

"Just a moment, Reverend Father," she said. "I'll be right back."

Jak gave me a big smile, clearly pleased with our preferential status. I doubt that any vendor had ever treated him in such a fashion, and he couldn't help but feel impressed with his own importance. I didn't begrudge him.

Mrs. Buboi returned with our noodles, two large bowls heaped with steaming noodles and broth, and placed them on the table between us.

"Mrs. Buboi, I need to-"

"Oh no," she said, interrupting me, "Reverend Father, you just eat your noodles first and then we'll talk. Look at the time!" She was gone before I could so much as respond.

I looked at the clock sitting on top of her large refrigerator: It was eight minutes to noon. That meant I had eight minutes to eat my noodles lest I wanted to break one of my vows, which I didn't.

Leave it to Mrs. Buboi to notice that.

"You better hurry," Jak said, as if we were committing some crime.

I needed no encouragement.

We don't have "commandments," as such, but we Buddhists do have our lists. Those starting off on the Buddhist path take up the Five Precepts — things like "don't kill", "don't lie", and "avoid illicit sex." Basic things, really, that one would expect from any decent person. If you want to deepen your practice, you can take three more precepts, one of which is not to eat food after 12 p.m. The other two are not to "sleep on a high bed" and not to attend "parties where there is music and dancing." Eight precepts are about as far as most lay people go. Buddhist nuns commonly take Ten Precepts. As a monk, I have the Patimokkha to think about, the 227 rules of conduct, plus another set of guidelines — hundreds in all — that while not strictly binding like the Patimokkha, were behaviors to strive after and faults to learn to avoid.

At any rate, the one about not eating after 12 p.m. was one of the foundational precepts, and I dared not break it. Thus, when noon came, I was nearly finished, but still I pushed the bowl away immediately. While Jak finished, I tried to savor the taste of the noodles in the back of my mouth. It was pathetic, of course, but I do like them, so there you are.

Mrs. Buboi showed up about five minutes after twelve, and nodded happily when she saw that I had kept my vows and that she hadn't been an occasion of sin for me. She picked up the bowls.

"Mrs. Buboi," I said. "You're busy, so I'll be quick. You've heard about the boy at our monastery?"

Her face clouded over with anguish. "Terrible, terrible," she said. "Very bad."

I stood up, trying to speak to her without looking at her, which wasn't always easy. "Are people in the neighborhood saying anything about the monastery, anything unusual?"

I glanced at her in time to catch the look of trepidation that passed across her ample features. She didn't want to answer. People usually don't when there wasn't anything good to be said.

"Please tell me," I said. "It's important. I think the boy's death had something to do with drugs."

"Oh dear," she said softly. "Well, I have heard some things, of course. We all do."

"What have you heard?"

She frowned, didn't want to answer.

I looked at Jak, who was standing and staring at the two of us. "Will you excuse us, Jak? I'll be right out."

He gave me that look of disapproval and hurt again and I wanted to crop his ears and tell him to stop taking everything so personally, but he left quickly, without protest, least none that anyone might see.

"No one will ever know," I said to her kindly. "You can say what you like, and my love for your noodles won't change."

"Oh Father Ananda!" she exclaimed. "It's not that. It's just that ... well, yes, we do hear things. About those boys, the ones hanging out there at the temple. The motorcycles. The deliveries. People are asking questions, wanting to know what they're doing. Folks say it's drugs, they're selling drugs, or delivering them. There was a story in Thai Rath, don't you know, about these kids making deliveries on their bikes. Not your kids, but some kids in Klong Toey, down there by the market. Got themselves mobile phones, they do, and the customer calls up and says what he wants, and off they go. Wearing new clothes, chains, got all sorts of money. I don't know, father. Me and my family, we worked hard all our lives, earned everything we ever got. But these kids — they want everything, and they don't want to work for it either. They just want to have their fun and wear their nice clothes and talk on their shiny phones. I don't know what it all means."

"So folks in the neighborhood think those kids are selling drugs?"

She nodded.

I thanked her, and joined Jak outside.

"Did you remember to pay?" I asked.

He looked guiltily at me.

"Go pay," I said. Mrs. Buboi would never think of charging a monk for a bowl of noodles, but when I had money, I insisted on paying, wary of the Yellow Tiger syndrome.

We returned to the monastery on foot, and as we passed through the gates, I took a rather long look at the boys congregated there, around their motorbikes, wondering how I was going to get to the bottom of things. Some of those boys were wearing nice clothes indeed, and I could see flashes of gold in the sunlight, gold on their wrists, gold around their necks, gold on their fingers.

If these kids were knee deep in illegal drugs, I was going to make them wish they weren't.

Six

I went to the main office.

"You forgot about those files," Kittisaro said accusingly. He had a stack of them on his desk. "For all the current kids."

"Got busy," I said. "You got a key for me?"

He handed over Brother Suchinno's key to the cage in the storage room and I pocketed it. It wasn't that I didn't trust Kittisaro ; it was simply best if no one else had the keys but me.

"Can I use one of your desks?" I asked.

He nodded.

He had several, with various pieces of computer equipment spread out here and there. I chose the least-cluttered desk and sat down.

"You know, if all of those files had been entered in a database, you could do your work faster. You could query your SQL, come up with answers in a snap. You could cross reference your tables, set up multiple indexes, query on a key word, stuff like that."

"Are you learning a foreign language?" I asked. "Because it's gobbledygook to me."

"Nothing foreign about it," he said. "Easy. A snap. I could do it, if you wanted."

I buried my nose in the files, hoping he wouldn't continue. Computer geeks made me feel incredibly stupid.

Nothing in the files on the boys seemed interesting. Each contained an application form for the program, which the boy had filled out on his first day, along with assessment reports from Brother Khantiphalo, and miscellaneous items — complaints, copies of correspondence to the boy's family, if any, and whatnot.

We had a lot of hotheaded kids on our hands, but nothing to suggest that any of them were murderers.

"What about notifying Brother Banditto's family?" I asked.

"The file's missing," Kittisaro said with a shrug.

"Missing?" I asked.

He shrugged again helplessly.

"What do you mean, *missing*?"

"It's gone," he said, his voice rising. "It's not in the filing cabinets. I looked yesterday." He sounded personally offended.

"Where are those cabinets?"

"In the abbot's office. He's the only who can look at them. I mean, you'd have to go into his office if you wanted to look at them."

"And the file for Brother Banditto is missing?"

For some reason, I found this hard to believe. If the file was missing, then we had no way of knowing whom Banditto was — who to notify, in case of emergency, where he was from, and so forth.

"That's rather inconvenient," I said at last.

Kittisaro cowered behind his computer. He always took things too personally, too seriously, as if everything was always his fault and the world was going to fall down on his shoulders if someone complained.

"You can stop cowering," I said. "No one's blaming you."

He progressed from cowering to pouting.

"Kittisaro, do you, by any chance, have a list of the monks in these computers of yours?"

"Of course I do."

"Could you print out a list of current monks, and compare them to the files in the abbot's office? I'd like to know if any other files are missing. I don't like those kinds of surprises."

"Do you know how long that's going to take?"

"Your lunar thing will have to wait. And I have one other thing to ask you."

"It's Linux, by the way."

I handed him the piece of paper I had found among Noi's things, the one with the threat written on it. I had enclosed it in plastic. "I need you to look at this carefully, and then compare the handwriting to the application forms in the files on the monks. I need to know who wrote this message."

"*Stop bothering me or else*?" he said, his face puzzled.

"Don't ask. When can you finish?"

"You want this done today?" he asked, surprised.

"Like, in the next hour or so."

"I'll get right on it. I hope they never make you the abbot."

"So do I," I said, smiling and leaving him to it.

Seven

My next chore was going to require help as well, so I went to fetch Jak again. I showed him the photographs of the footprints in the bathroom. A pair of flip-flops or sandals with a distinctive tread pattern had made them. They were faint, but the tread patterns were visible.

All we had to do was check the shoes and sandals of about 250 or so people to see if we could find a match.

"You're joking," Jak said, the look on his face one of bleak horror.

"I'm not," I said.

"This could take forever."

"Well, we'd better get started then."

In the afternoons, most monks were meditating either in their kutis or cells, or attending classes of one sort or another — learning Pali, or chants, or memorizing sutras, or listening to religious instruction given by one of the senior monks. This would make our job a bit easier, although we would most likely miss a few pairs of shoes here and there.

We went round to the kutis first, stopping in front of each, examining the shoes that were placed in front of it. We received many looks and inquiries from the monks, but no one seemed unduly stressed by it. From there we went to the main dormitory, and sorted through the mountain of shoes at the entranceways, comparing likely candidates against the photographs we had, but not finding anything particularly relevant. We went around to the different classes in the different buildings, wherever we could find shoes piled out front. After two hours, it was obvious we weren't getting anywhere. There were some similar matches, but not convincingly so. We came across nothing that we could consider an exact match. It was frustrating and time-consuming, and I had never looked at the bottoms of so many pairs of shoes in my life.

The heat of the day was up, and I was getting angry at our lack of progress. The skies above us were overcast, promising — teasing — but not yet ready to deliver the rains they held. As the days went by it would become muggier and more uncomfortable until the rainy season began at last.

"Is this what the police have to do every day?" Jak asked, glancing at me after picking up another pair of shoes.

"If they have to," I said.

"It must be boring."

"It is."

EIGHT

I went to the main office to see Kittisaro .

"What have you got for me?" I asked.

Kittisaro, despite himself, was enjoying the task I'd given him. It was probably a bit more exciting than the Linux thing.

"Three possible matches," he said proudly, handing me three files. He came out from behind his receptionist's desk and stood by my side, grinning and excited. "Did the killer write this note?" he asked.

"Not likely," I said. "But then again, who knows?"

I opened the files. He pointed out the similarities in the writing, the way some letters resembled each other, but there was no clear, exact match.

"Now, what have you overlooked?" I asked.

He looked at the three files, his face screwed up in concentration.

"What do you mean?" he asked.

"Whom was the note signed by?"

He read it again.

"Someone named *C*."

"Do you suppose that would be Brother Chittakhutto, as opposed to Brother Panyathiro and Brother Phalathammo?"

He grinned with embarrassment.

"Could you summon Brother Chittakhutto please?"

He went back around his desk and got on the phone, and about three minutes later Brother Chittakhutto showed up at the main office, a look of consternation on his face.

I took him by the arm and led him outside. I wanted a bit of privacy. We went to one of the concrete benches in front, near the parking lot. This one was beneath a large, shady tree. Our only companions were the several dogs lounging in the shade.

I handed him the note and asked him if he had written it.

I didn't need his reply to know that he had. His eyes went wide, his lower lip trembled, and he wouldn't give me his eyes.

"Would you care to explain?" I asked.

He put his hands together in his lap, taking in a deep breath. He was a rather handsome brother, youngish, perhaps mid-twenties or so. He seemed delicate, more of a poet than a construction worker, more of a scholar than a murderer. And as I looked at this file it became clear that he was a scholar indeed, moving up the Buddhist study ladder quite readily, to the point where he was now being considered for a royal title. That would put him squarely in the rising star category, and he must have worked very hard to get where he was at.

"I knew you were going to come looking for me," he said, his eyes staring at the ground. "I didn't hurt that boy."

I waited.

At last, he did give me his eyes, as if trying to judge how I was going to react to what he had to say.

"Nong Noi used to come to my kuti. The first time was at night. It was past the final bell. I had lain down and was going to sleep. He just came right in, opened the door, and walked into my kuti. Said he needed to talk to someone. I tried to get him to leave, but he seemed so sad and so hurt about something, so I let him stay. Next thing I know he's taking his clothes off and wants to lie down with me. I tried to stop him, but I couldn't. I was afraid we were going to rouse attention. I didn't know what to do. So he just took his clothes off and got in my bed, and covered himself up with the blanket. I asked him what he wanted to talk about. He said there was nothing to say. He just wanted to be with someone. He just wanted someone to hold him. I didn't know what to do."

He looked at the ground, shaking his head.

All sorts of alarm bells were going off in my mind.

"You had never talked to him before this?" I asked.

He shook his head. "Not really. I'd seen him, of course. He'd come up to me once or twice, wanting to talk, but I put him off. I didn't like him, to be honest. He was pushy, aggressive, a bit of a pest."

"And then one night, he goes to your kuti? Just shows up?"

Chittakhutto nodded. "Ananda, I didn't kill that boy. I know what it looks like, but I didn't kill him."

He gave me a helpless look, a sort of deer-in-the-headlights look.

"So what happened?" I asked.

He didn't want to answer, and didn't, not for a long time. "He was naked, in my bed. I didn't know what to do. Go get the abbot? Wake everybody up and say there's a naked boy in my bed? I was embarrassed. And I felt bad for him. He just wanted someone to hold him. He kept begging me to just lie down and hold him. I told him to put his clothes on, and I would. So he did. He put his shorts back on. So I laid down, and I tried to hold him. And then he told me he was going to kill himself, that nobody loved him, his family had rejected him, he had nowhere to go, his life was miserable — you know, all of that stuff. So I tried to tell him that suicide wasn't the answer, but he didn't want to hear it. And then he started crying, and it just went on and on. And finally, I fell asleep. The next morning he was gone. But then he came again, that night, and I told him he couldn't stay, that he shouldn't be visiting my kuti, that he had no right. But he wouldn't listen. He told me stop him, if I thought I could. And then he said a lot of bad things to me, about how mean all the monks were, how selfish we were, what a bunch of losers we were, how we didn't care about anybody but ourselves.

"I'm telling you, Ananda, it was a nightmare. And he kept doing it, every night. And I should have said something to the abbot, but I didn't want to get him in trouble. But after a while I couldn't stand it anymore. He was so full of self-pity, and he was so angry, and he hated everyone, but he wanted everyone to love him, and he couldn't understand why nobody did.

"So finally, I went to talk to Brother Khantiphalo, and I told him about it. I had to find some way to make it stop. So Brother Khantiphalo talked to him, and he didn't come around — for a while. But then he started again, sometimes during the day. I would come back to my kuti after breakfast and he would be in there, sitting on my bed, naked, like he was taunting me. So one day I'd had enough, and I left him there and went to get the abbot. When we came back, he was gone. But then he came that night. So I wrote this note, and left it on my door, and went to sleep in the main dormitory instead for a while, to get away from him. So he must have found it, and kept it."

Chittakhutto looked at me. He seemed like he was on the verge of tears. "I didn't kill him, Father Ananda. You have to believe me."

I tried to picture the scene in my mind, and I felt sorry for both him and Nong Noi. The boy's behavior was pathetic, but it spoke of a desperate need for love, for someone to care. Maybe that's all our boys really needed — someone to care. Why was that so hard to do? As Buddhists, we tried to have compassion for all beings, humans, cats, dogs, even mosquitoes and messed up kids. We tried to train ourselves to wish that everyone be happy, be free from suffering. We tried to apply the medicine of the Buddha's teachings to whatever wounds we encountered.

Easier said than done, of course.

"Do you have any idea who killed this boy?" I asked.

Chittakhutto frowned and shook his head.

"Did you see him with anyone else?" I asked.

He put his face in his hands, sighing. For a long moment, he sat there like that, holding his face in his hands, sighing. "I saw him, sometimes, hanging around the other kutis."

"Whose?" I asked.

He didn't want to answer, but I needed to know.

"Brother Satchapalo," he said at last.

"Did you ever see him with Brother Banditto?" I asked, on a hunch.

"I saw them walking together once, leaving the temple and going somewhere."

"Did they seem friendly to you?"

He shrugged.

"How long ago was Noi visiting your kuti?"

"It was a couple of months ago."

"And he didn't bother you afterwards?"

"Sometimes he'd look at me, if I was out in front. One time he gave me the middle finger. I ignored it. But no, he didn't bother me after that."

"Is there anything else you should be telling me?" I asked. Open-ended questions were always good, if only to judge the body language they provoked. In this case, I could see there was more to the story than what I'd heard. He put a hand to his lips, as to stop whatever wanted to come out. He seemed embarrassed.

"Is there?" I asked.

"You mean, did I break my vows?" He turned to look at me, his eyes full of fear and sorrow.

I considered that for a moment. That wasn't what I had meant. But I could see what he was getting at.

"That isn't my business," I said.

There were, of course, offences for which a monk was instantly defrocked. He could continue wearing the robes and pretending, but he was no longer a monk and nothing he did as a monk had any merit whatsoever. But not all offenses were that serious, and most could be remedied.

"That's between you and the abbot," I said, "and if you haven't talked to him about it, you should. If you've done something you ought not to have done, you might be able to do penance. There are ways to repair the damage. But that's not my business, and it's not what I meant. What I meant was, have you seen anything suspicious about this boy? Anyone he was hanging around, anyone he was bothering, anything that might have gotten him killed?"

He shook his head. "I'm not a suspect, am I?" he asked.

I wasn't going to break my vows by lying, so I said, simply, "Yes. So far, you're the only one. You. And Brother Banditto. But not a strong suspect, and I doubt very much that you did it."

I left him with his thoughts.

Nine

Brother Satchapalo was a tall man, his arms thick with muscle, his face framed with the sort of hardness I always associated with drug addicts and others living on the edge. And yet, despite his appearance, he was a calm, cultured man, who kept himself well in hand.

He was sitting on the steps to his kuti. I was standing at the foot of the steps, watching him. I had asked him whether he had had any contact with Nong Noi.

He shrugged. "I knew him."

When he didn't elaborate, I asked him to.

He shrugged again. "I saw him around, like everyone, I guess."

"Did he ever come to your kuti?" I asked.

He gave me a long look before nodding.

"And what did he want?"

"The bloody idiot came to my kuti one night and wanted to sleep with me."

I waited for him to elaborate, but he did not.

"Wanted to sleep with you?"

"Crying in his beer about something. The kid was a loser."

"So what did you do?"

"I told him to get out."

I waited, but Satchapalo was not about to be drawn, not about to rush in and fill up the empty silences with a rush of words. He was a careful man, I thought.

"So did he?" I asked, when the silence had grown too long.

"Course he did," Satchapalo said, looking up to me. "I'm not his bloody mother."

That was certainly true.

"Did he pester you? Keep coming around? Do anything strange?"

He shook his head.

"Why do you think he came to you that first time?"

"He was crackers, Ananda. Who knows why those people do what they do?"

"Crackers?"

"Well, you don't just bloody go to someone's house at night and take your clothes and crawl in their bed, do you?"

"So he took his clothes off?"

Satchapalo nodded.

"And that bothered you?"

"Of course it did. You think I'm a faggot or something?"

"So what did you do?"

He was getting impatient now. "I told him to bloody well get out of my kuti. I took his clothes and threw them out the front door and told him to follow."

"And did he?"

He gave me an angry look, as if none of this was my business. "What does it matter?" he asked.

"I need to know what happened."

"You think I killed the idiot?"

"I didn't say that. I just need to know what happened that night."

He was angry. I could see it in the tenseness of his body, the hard set to his face, the way he clenched his teeth together.

"I grabbed him by the arm, pushed him out the door, and told him to bugger off."

"And was it just this one time?"

He nodded.

"He didn't come back afterward, didn't bother you again?"

He shook his head.

"Do you have any idea who might have killed him, or why?"

"He was a bloody idiot, wasn't he?"

"It sounds that way. But we don't kill people because they're annoying. Do we?"

"Well, someone did," he said, "didn't they? But it wasn't me."

By the time I'd finished with Brother Satchapalo, he was No. 1 on my list of suspects. And yet I had to remind myself that the most likely explanation for Nong Noi's death was that Brother Banditto had killed him, and then fled the scene, and that just because someone has annoyed you doesn't mean you're going to kill them.

Well, not always.

Ten

I had one more thing to do that day, and my footsteps now took me to the boys' dormitory in search of Brother Khantiphalo. I wanted to talk to him about what I'd heard Mrs. Nuan and Mrs. Buboi discussing — that his boys were "selling something."

"Selling something?" he repeated, outraged, when I had explained my conversations with the two women. "What do you mean, selling something?"

"That's what I'm asking you, Brother Khantiphalo. I don't know. Do you have any idea what they're talking about?"

"The boys have to be in by 6 p.m., dinnertime. We have some evening activities and they go to bed. After breakfast in the morning, they're free to go and do what they like. Some of them have part-time jobs. Some of them run errands. Some of them go hang out in the park. Who knows? I mean, I can't control them all day long. I don't know what they're doing, to be honest. I have to watch over the ones who stay, usually about twenty or so. We go help out in the laundry or the kitchen or something. Sometimes we go to the park ourselves. If there's some money, we might go out to eat. But the ones who don't stay during the day, I can't really say — I don't know what they do."

"So it's possible," I said, "that some of them are indeed selling drugs, or something like that?"

He didn't like the thought of that. But he nodded his head. "And anyway, you know how these women are. They read something like that in Thai Rath and then they think everyone's doing it. Of course, I'll keep my eyes open and see if anything's going on, but I really doubt it, Father Ananda. I mean, come on, this is a temple here — these kids can't be selling drugs in broad daylight. We lock the gates at night, so they can't be coming and going, unless they're climbing over the wall. But my bed is right by the door in the dormitory, and if they so much as fart in their sleep, I'd know it."

"I'm just telling you what I heard," I said. Brother Khantiphalo took his program very seriously, and I hadn't meant to get him all worked up.

"I know you are, but if these kids are doing something like that, they could ruin the funding for my program. And anyway, I don't see how they could be getting away with something like that when I've been working so hard to stay on top on things."

"Maybe you need help," I suggested.

"Maybe I do," he replied. And then he grinned. "You interested?"

No, I was most certainly not. "Keep an eye on them," I said, "and let me know if you come across anything that's suspicious."

Eleven

On my way back to my kuti — and a bit of well-deserved rest — I stopped by to see Brother Kittisaro again.

"Got a list for you," he said.

"A list?"

"You asked me to see if any of the other files were missing. Some are. Four of them, to be exact."

He handed me a list of names, and I stared at them, intrigued. Along with the file for Brother Banditto, we had somehow managed to misplace files for Brother Panyathiro, Brother Chutintharo, and — I was a bit surprised — Brother Satchapalo.

The list was rather disturbing, for I had often seen some of these brothers together, especially Chutintharo and Satchapalo. Banditto had often kept company with Panyathiro, and sometimes Chutintharo. In fact, the more I thought about it, the more I realized that I had often seen these particular brothers together, sometimes sitting on a bench out front, sometimes leaving the monastery together, sometimes sitting together in the prayer hall. One of them was now missing, and another one was my favorite suspect in the death of one of our boys.

Coincidence?

I had never believed in coincidence, and wasn't about to do so now.

"Thanks, Kittisaro ," I said, giving him a smile.

"Does it mean something to you?" he asked.

"It could," I said.

Twelve

At 3 p.m., I was sitting in one of the salas, cross-legged on the floor, in front of four of our boys, preparing to lead them in a meditation.

We sat on cushions, in the proper position, hands in our laps.

Sitting directly in front of me was Bin, a fifteen-year-old from the South, dark-skinned, already ravaged by years of first sniffing glue and then graduating to *yaa baa*, or speed, and then ecstasy, when he could get it, not to mention copious amounts of whiskey and other alcoholic beverages. Though fifteen, he looked much older, and his eyes had a haunted look to them. Beneath them were brown bags, giving his eyes a hollowed out look. He was wearing a tank top and shorts, and was little more than skin and bones.

Sitting to the left of him was Yok, a seventeen-year-old from Chon Buri, who had drifted into Bangkok, the way so many others had, looking for excitement. He'd found plenty of it. A good-looking boy, he had gone to work at a brothel catering to a male clientele. For two years he had sold his body and used his money to buy heroin — the insides of his arms were testament to that, with their many needle marks, not to mention the veins on his ankles and elsewhere. He'd gotten himself so addicted that the money he made wasn't enough to pay for his drugs, and he began stealing from his clients, one of whom beat him to within an inch of his life and had left him for dead in an alley. His subsequent hospital stay turned up the fact that he was now HIV-positive. Though apparently in good health, that could change any day, and he would begin his gradual decline into AIDS and die from it, the way so many thousands of others already had.

The afternoon heat and humidity was making all of us uncomfortable, and Yok had removed his shirt and was now sitting, dressed in shorts, eyeing me with annoyance, his dark eyes conveying words his lips wouldn't dare say.

The other two were similar to Bin and Yok, haunted young men, coming from troubled pasts, trying to cope with addictions that had gotten out of hand, addictions which they no longer had any money to pay for.

"What happened to Nong Noi?" Bin asked, before we got started.

"He's dead," I said.

"I know that," Bin replied, rolling his eyes. "I mean, what happened to him?"

"I don't know," I said. "The matter is being looked into."

"Like anyone cares," Yok said, sneering at me.

"I care," I said quietly.

He made a face and took his eyes away from me.

We had an electric fan blowing, slowly revolving on its base, but it wasn't enough to chase off the humidity. It was mid-July and the rainy season was getting ready to begin. Each day the air got heavier with anticipation, and the afternoons were especially difficult. If a breeze picked up and blew the air around, it was bearable, but today there was no breeze, only the weak output of our tiny fan, and I could see the boys were just as irritated and unhappy as I was.

"Let's begin," I said. "What we're trying to do today is just be aware, just have some awareness, of what you're feeling, or what you're thinking. That's all we're going to do. When you find yourself aware of something, I want you to say to yourself, I'm aware of hunger. I'm aware of the heat. I'm aware of a feeling of anger. That's all."

We sat in silence for long moments.

"I'm aware that I'm horny," Yok said, provoking laughter from the other boys.

When they quieted down, I did not reprimand him. "That's good," I said, and he looked at me rather oddly, as if he wasn't hearing correctly. "You're aware of the desire for sex. Sex is a powerful drive, a powerful emotion. None of us are immune. So you're aware of that. That's good. For the next five minutes, let's just sit here. If you're aware of sex, fine. That's reality. You're not going to get up and go chasing after someone to have sex. You're just going to sit here and be aware of that feeling. If you're hungry, you're aware of your hunger. You're not going to jump up and run to the kitchen to get something to eat. You're just going to sit here and be aware that you're hungry. That's all."

"It's stupid," Yok said.

"It's never stupid to be aware of what you're feeling, of what you're doing, of what might be going on inside you."

"Yes," he said, "but what difference does it make? So you're aware of it. So what."

"Most people aren't aware of themselves," I replied evenly. "They just do things, and they don't know why. They don't know what's going on inside of them, or why they do the things they do. Addiction to drugs is a good example. Why do you need drugs? Why do you put yourself at risk to get them? When you see that they're hurting your body, why don't you stop?"

"I could use some drugs," Yok said, lowering his eyes.

"So you just say, I'm aware of this need for drugs. That's all. It doesn't mean you have to get up and go get some. You're just trying to train yourself to be aware of what you're doing."

"But why?" he asked, and I could tell he was genuinely curious and wanting to know.

"Because," I said, "when you're aware of yourself, of what you're doing, of what you want, or how you feel, then you can begin to make choices. You feel hunger. So you can say to yourself, alright, I'm hungry. I can get up and go eat something. Or I can wait. I can make a choice about it. I'm not an animal. I don't have to satisfy all my cravings immediately. I can decide on an appropriate course of action."

"And how it that going to help me?" he asked.

The others were quiet, listening very carefully, also interested to know my response.

"It's about suffering," I said. "You and I are no different. We both live in the same world. We are both exposed to the same things each day. You're joking about being horny. Do you think monks never experience sexual attractions and desires? Do you think you're the only ones addicted to some substance or other? For you it may be heroin. For me, it may be coffee. I may be unhappy when I can't have it. I may be miserable, withdrawn, angry, desperate for my coffee. I may be addicted to cigarettes. I may be addicted to peace and quiet, and find myself getting angry each time a dog barks or someone disturbs me. But the point is, whatever the addiction, it can't be dealt with until you know you're addicted, until you know what you're doing, how this addiction process works. And each and every day, you have to cope with the craving to satisfy your addiction. So when you teach yourself to be aware, to be aware of what you're feeling and what you're doing, you can begin to teach yourself to be on your guard. When you start feeling that addiction flare up, you can stand back, you can be careful, you can make decisions about it. You don't just have to do it. You know you can make a choice about it."

They considered this silently.

"Are you all happy right now?" I asked.

They laughed at me.

"Why not?" I asked. When they didn't respond, I plodded on, hoping I was making sense, hoping they might get the point. "You're not happy because you got yourself involved with drugs, and you've learned the hard way about how painful drugs can be. If you knew that one day you would be sitting here, having to listen to me, would you have gotten involved in the

first place? If you knew what awaited you? If you knew how hard it would be to stop taking these drugs?"

There was a general shaking of heads.

"So what we're trying to do is, first of all, be aware. Be mindful of what you're doing, of the consequences that an action can have. Be mindful of the fact that you have choices you can make. You can get involved in something, or you can decide not to get involved. You can begin to realize that some things that we do create suffering and unhappiness, and then you can begin to stop doing those things that create suffering and unhappiness. And pretty soon, you'll begin to see that when you stop creating suffering for yourself, you'll stop suffering. You'll learn how to make better decisions and choices. You'll learn that bad actions lead to bad consequences, and good actions will lead to good consequences. You'll begin to see that if you're unhappy, you're the one who made yourself that way, and you can stop it, you can do things differently and get a different outcome. But it all has to start here, with being aware of yourself, aware of what you're feeling, of what's going on inside you."

We sat again in silence for about a minute.

Bin, sitting in front of me, began crying, and his face was quickly contorted into pain and unhappiness.

I said nothing. It was perfectly okay for them to cry — most of them did eventually.

"Now let's just sit here for about five minutes," I said quietly. "If you're feeling unhappy, that's fine. Just be aware of that. If you want to cry, go right ahead. But let's just sit here and be aware of what we're doing, for just five minutes."

While Bin was crying, the boy sitting next to him, an eighteen-year-old from the outskirts of Bangkok, began shaking. He was holding his hands together in his lap, in the proper fashion, but his arms and legs were trembling. His eyes were squeezed shut and he was biting at his bottom lip.

When confronted with the cold, hard fact of their addiction, of their desire for drugs, most of the boys did similar things: Shake, or clench their hands into fists, or get angry, or cry. Some started arguments. Some got up and ran away. There was very often shame involved — if not shame, then blame. The mind wanted to blame someone else for its misfortune. The mind wanted a target. But in the end it had to come to a point where the boy could sit down, and be with that shame or blame, and not get up and run away from it, but face it.

We sat in silence for many minutes, and I glanced occasionally at their faces, surprised by their earnestness. After about ten minutes I quietly brought them out of this meditative state, complimenting them for their effort and telling them they were free to leave.

They did. But Yok remained behind, and I could tell, by the look on his face, that he had something to say and wasn't sure he could bring himself to say it.

The expression in his eyes pained me. It was that look I had seen so often, that of a child drowning, wondering if I was the one who could save him, the one who could reach out a hand and pull him up from the depths.

He wiped at his eyes, as if he thought he might start crying. His lips were moving but he couldn't bring himself to say what he wanted to say.

"What is it?" I asked quietly.

He looked at me and bit at his lower lip. "Do you really care?" he asked.

It was a strange question, and yet one I had heard many times before. Most of these kids had come from broken homes, had experienced bad things at the hands of parents and adults, and sometimes needed to be reassured that there were adults who did "care," a sort of all-encompassing word they used to mean not just caring about them personally, but also to suggest that I was a safe adult, was not going to hurt them, would take their feelings seriously, and wouldn't mock them or abandon them the way other adults had.

"What do you mean?" I asked, wanting to draw him out.

He lowered his eyes. "It's just that I'm going to die, and I don't want to die." He said this very quietly, and he was referring to his being HIV-positive.

"You're not going to die anytime soon," I said. "And if you don't want to die, then start taking care of yourself. Start thinking about your health. Stay away from cigarettes and alcohol. Stay away from drugs. Eat good food. Get a lot of exercise. You don't have the rest of your life ahead of you. But you do have five years, or ten years, or maybe even more. That's something, isn't it? And the more you take care of yourself now, the more time you'll have."

This wasn't what he wanted to hear, but I didn't know what else to tell him.

I frowned, feeling bad for him, knowing that sometimes there wasn't anything that could be said, that what these boys really wanted was for someone to put an arm around their shoulder and tell them everything was going to be alright, even if that was a lie.

"I'm going to meditate some more," he said, putting his face in his hands. His shoulders were shaking and I knew he was trying to stop himself from crying.

"I'll sit with you," I said. "We can meditate together."

He didn't respond, but rather, for a long time, sat with his face in his hands, crying softly, wiping at his eyes, thoroughly miserable.

Then, without a word, he got up and left.

Thirteen

By the time I took my place for the 4 p.m. funeral chants for Nong Noi, I was exhausted, emotionally drained. Too many things were reminding me of my past, of my own pain, of things I preferred not to think about.

The chanting was a sad affair. Nong Noi was in his coffin, up on the saw-horse pedastals. The easel standing to the side of the coffin, which was supposed to hold a picture of the deceased, was empty — there was no framed picture of Noi that could be used for this purpose. To the other side of the coffin, there were more easels, these ones to hold the flower arrangements brought by mourners, and these too were empty. In the middle of the sala with its large couch, where parents and family should be sitting, there was nothing but an empty couch.

No mourners had come.

No one was interested in the death of this boy. No one was mourning his passing, unless they had been forced to, like the monks and the dek wats, the temple boys.

CHAPTER THREE

"Be on your guard against physical agitation; be controlled in body. Forsaking bodily misconduct, follow right conduct in body."

The Lord Buddha. From the Dhammapada, #231.

One

I went through my morning routine, trying to be mindful of what I was doing. If walking, to be mindful that I was walking. If dressing, to be mindful I was dressing. If chanting, to be mindful I was chanting — all just as Brother Thammarato had taught me when I had first arrived at Wat Mahanat so many years ago. Simple stuff, really, but important.

I had the sense that all the pieces of the puzzle — to the murder of the boy, but also to my life in general — were right in front of my eyes. All it required on my part was a bit of mindfulness and awareness, a bit of observation, a willingness to be still and let the pieces come together of their own accord.

During the morning chant and meditation session, I allowed my mind to become free of thought, following along with the sonorous Pali words, and then sitting in silence, enjoying the ritual for what it was — calming, soothing, quieting.

Afterward, we lined up to go on our alms round. I lingered in the prayer hall, allowing time for the other monks to line up, some with their kuti boys, others alone, and when it was almost time to go, I walked slowly to my place in line.

Then I observed an unusual scene: Brothers Satchapalo, Chutintharo and Panyathiro each had kuti boys, and those boys were the better dressed, the ones with flashy sneakers and wristwatches. Those three brothers also just happened to be the ones, along with the now missing Brother Banditto, whose files had "disappeared."

Coincidence?

Didn't believe in them.

I took my place in line, allowing this information to register.

Jak appeared and stood at my side, carrying a yellow plastic bucket, offering me a small smile. The gates to the temple opened and we began to file out.

The three brothers, I noted, were light-skinned, like Brother Banditto, suggesting they were all from the North, but the similarities ended there. Brother Satchapalo was handsome, in an odd sort of way, with full lips and a strong jaw. He was tall and muscular. Behind him was Brother Chutintharo, a short fellow with a pinched face and eyes that always seemed to be hiding something or laughing at something — or someone. And behind him was Brother Panyathiro, on the husky side, but strong, like an ox, with a round face and a large nose.

I watched the three brothers, and their kuti boys, as they turned left on the main road. Jak and I normally turned right and went in the opposite direction. This morning, I was going to follow my instincts.

I turned left.

"Father Ananda?" Jak said, frowning at me.

"Come along," I whispered.

He gave me a confused look — we were deviating from established practice again, and he didn't like it. But he said nothing as we walked along slowly, keeping a fair bit of distance from the three brothers — for some reason, I was now thinking of them as the Gang of Three — who soon separated themselves from the other monks, continuing on along the main road until they turned into a small side street, all of them together.

That was odd.

"What are they doing?" Jak asked.

That was a perfect question to ask. It wasn't our normal practice to go on our rounds together. We each took a separate route.

"That's what we're going to find out," I said.

We walked quickly until we got to the mouth of the alley.

"Stick your head around the corner there and see where they are," I said to Jak. "But don't let them see you."

Traffic was on the main road was light, but picking up. Old folks were out in force, getting in morning walks before the streets and sidewalks became too clogged with vendors and pedestrians and vehicles. What they thought of a middle-aged monk and his kuti boy standing in a doorway, I could only guess.

Jak walked slowly to the corner, which was the end of a long row of shop houses that looked to be like an auto repair business. I watched his hitched walk, the way he had to rise up on his good leg and then sink down on his bad one. He paused at the corner of the shop house and slowly put his head around the corner, and remained that way for long moments. Then he turned back to me, motioning for me to go see for myself.

I peered around the corner. The Gang was about halfway down the alley, collecting offerings. Afraid we would lose sight of them, I said, "Jak, follow them, but stay behind and don't let them see you. When they turn off into another street, just wait for me, okay?"

He nodded and made to go, but I took hold of his arm. "If they see you — if you think you're in any sort of danger — you just yell and make a fuss and run. You understand?"

"I can take care of myself," he said, giving me an imperious look.

He moved into the alley, filled with shop houses and small stores selling cigarettes and sweets, or paper products, or food.

There were vendors lined up with their carts, already in full swing, servicing the morning crowds. It provided plenty of opportunity for Jak to hide or linger and not arouse too much suspicion.

I followed myself, when the Gang of Three had gotten a good ways down the alley. I kept myself hidden behind vendor carts or parked cars, and received numerous odd looks from passers-by.

I ventured from out behind the back of a large SUV and saw that the monks had disappeared. I walked quickly down the crowded street and found Jak waiting for me.

"They went down there," he said, pointing to a side street down and to the right.

I nodded.

We followed, and again Jak went on ahead to peek around the corner. But this time, he looked back to me and shrugged, holding his hands up in the air, as if to say there was nothing to see.

I looked for myself. The Gang had vanished.

This street was a dead end, about fifty meters in length, with a few houses on one side, a row of shop houses on the other.

"Let's get out of here," I said, and I took the lead, retracing our footsteps back up the alley and out onto the main street. There was nothing more we could do at the moment, but it was interesting indeed that these three brothers had made a half-hearted attempt to collect alms and had then disappeared into a private residence.

I would have to return some other time when I wasn't wearing bright orange robes that screamed for attention.

Two

After breakfast, Jak hurried off to school and I positioned myself in the front of the monastery. Here and there was the odd concrete bench, most under the shade of trees, used most often by visitors or nearby office workers who brought their lunches and close friends.

I chose a bench in the back that allowed me to watch the comings and goings at the gate, the food vendors, Mrs. Nuan among them, as well as the boys congregated around their motorcycles. I brought along a dharma book, which I pretended to read. I also had a pad of paper and a pencil to make notes.

Life at an inner-city temple and monastery complex is not quiet. In the old days, out in the countryside, the temple was the heart of the community, there for spiritual as much as practical reasons. You could go there to learn meditation from the monks, if you liked, or to trade vegetables or sell dried-out fish. Weddings were held there, temple fairs, puppet shows, and traditional dances — if there was anything going on in the village, it would be happening at the temple.

Some of that spirit survives despite the modern setting. For many folks, the temple is still the heart of the community, and does not belong exclusively to the orange-clad monks who live in it, but to the people who support it and rely on it for spiritual sustenance and a sense of community and belonging.

I was reminded of these things as I watched folks coming and going. A line of vendors had set themselves up along the wall by the gate. They were the same vendors who arrived each morning. Mrs. Nuan, wearing her lampshade hat, sold fruits — pineapple, watermelon, Thai apples, and the like. Another woman sold fried doughnuts, popular in the mornings — most folks liked to eat them while drinking their morning cup of coffee. Another sold skewers of fried pork and chicken. Another sold drinks, cokes and sprites, but also iced coffees and guava juice.

Customers came through the gates, congregating around the vendors' carts, making their purchases and hurrying off to work or school — a fair number of the customers were kids, young and old, in their school uniforms, buying their morning snacks or breakfasts.

On the other side of the entrance gates was the motorcycle taxi stand, a line of about twelve bikes, each belching more black smoke than the last. A variety of down-on-their-luck types took up roost here — driving a motorcycle taxi was about as low on Bangkok's economic ladder as you could possibly get. Most of the drivers were either very young, late teens or early twenties, or very old – laid-off workers, others who couldn't get regular jobs or were no longer employable. A fair amount appeared perpetually drunk, or on the way. I wasn't sure how often they showered or changed their clothes, though I suspected those were luxuries they couldn't always afford.

Motorcycle taxis were good for short distances, for weaving through traffic chaos to get somewhere quickly. One required a certain steely resolve and the ability to keep one's eyes closed to ride them; motorcycle taxi guys take chances most prudent drivers would never dream of.

They arranged themselves in a line, and customers came, from time to time, needing lifts.

Just beyond that was the area where some of the boys from our temple congregated. I made a note of the names of the boys hanging out there for future reference. They had two motorcycles in their midst, and at least one had a mobile phone — an older boy who had dyed his hair red. I could not see this boy very well, but he did not strike me as anyone I had ever seen before. He might not be one of our boys at all. And if he wasn't, I wanted to know what he was doing at our temple.

There was a fair bit of coming and going of monks into this scene, some on their way out of the gates for business in the city, others hanging around on the benches or talking to the vendors or the motorcycle taxi guys.

Dogs were also in abundance, of course. They were most active in the mornings, but when the heat of the day came up, they — like the rest of us — quieted down and sought out shade and leisure.

There was work to do, of course, and each monk had his assigned tasks. Most of these tasks involved cleaning of one sort or another, in one building or another. Others took brooms and tackled the parking lots, or rakes to go after the never-ending supply of leaves and debris that littered the grounds.

While the morning and evening chanting sessions were mandatory for all monks, during the day the brothers were allowed to pursue their own forms of meditation and spiritual practice. Some took long walks around the complex, walking very slowly and mindfully, usually clutching beads. Others found quiet spots to sit and do nothing but be mindful — I was doing that, at the moment. Others attended classes or devoted themselves to learning chants or studying Pali and Sanskrit. The more advanced and older monks made themselves available for meditation classes, either for the younger monks or lay people.

Brothers like Suchinno had actual jobs: Seeing to maintenance, in his case, or preparing meals, or overseeing the laundry, or tending to the paperwork, or teaching in the grade school.

After about an hour of sitting, I got to my feet, collecting my book and pad of paper. I walked slowly through the parking lot. No one paid my any attention. I went over to where the boys were sitting congregated around their two motorcycles.

I addressed myself to the youth with red hair. "Do I know you?"

The boys quieted and regarded me with suspicious looks.

The red-haired boy shrugged.

"Then what you are doing at my temple?"

He gave a surprised, bewildered sort of look that suggested he couldn't believe what he was hearing.

"Just hanging out," he said.

"What do you do for a living?"

He frowned. "Like, a job?"

I nodded.

"Don't have no job," he said, smirking.

"Do you go to school?"

"I used to."

"What's your name?"

"Noot."

I gave him a long, appraising look. What was Noot doing at my temple? I looked around to the other boys. They were sheepish, embarrassed.

"Are you waiting for something?" I asked.

"Just hanging out."

"Why don't you go hang out somewhere else, Noot?"

A look of anger flashed across his features. He did not like being told what to do.

"It's not your business," he remarked, not looking at me.

I looked at the other youths. There were four of them. I asked for their names. They were Bee, Yut, Nin, and Cherd.

"All of you go over to the dining hall and wait there for me," I said.

Two of them got to their feet. The other two gave me insolent looks, as if they could not believe I was ordering them around.

"Do it now," I said.

There was a general sputtering and murmuring as they got to their feet and left.

Noot looed at me with contempt.

"Whose bikes are these?" I asked.

"Wouldn't know."

"Really?"

"Really," he said, sneering.

"Tell you what, Noot. Get on one of these bikes and get out of my monastery and don't let me see you here again."

"You can't do that," he said. The sneer was replaced by a look of genuine puzzlement.

"Yes, I can, because I just did it."

He looked around as if to see whether anyone had witnessed his humiliation, or if reinforcements might be arriving.

"You can't do this," he said with an angry snarl. "You're not the boss here."

I didn't answer, merely waited for him to accept the inevitable.

I heard footsteps behind me and turned to see Brother Suchinno, who came to a stop just beside me, putting a hand on my arm.

"You having trouble here?" he asked, and I wasn't sure which one of us he was addressing.

"I was just asking our young friend here to leave," I said, looking at him.

He gave me a small smile, turned to the boy. "Well, what are you waiting for? Off with you!"

The boy snorted, shaking his head back and forth as we were complete idiots. He jumped on one of the bikes, kick-started it, and snarled over his shoulder, "We'll see about this."

And off he went.

"Thanks," I said, turning to Suchinno.

"Not a problem," Suchinno answered. "Now, do you want to tell me why you're kicking people out, or should I go about my business and pretend like I didn't see what you just did?"

"Do you pay much attention to these kids?"

"They're a real pain sometimes. I don't know who some of them are, or what they're doing here, why they hang out here — who knows? I've never thrown any of them out, but I'd like to. This Noot fellow, he makes deliveries or something, and the boys come over and talk to him. He's a real talker, too, but they all get real quiet and secretive when I come around, so I know they're up to no good. That's why I was watching you, saw you come over here, thought you might need some help."

I thanked him again.

I went to find the young men I had sent to the dining hall. They were sitting on the floor in a circle, appropriately quiet and sheepish, as if I had caught them doing something wrong.

Had I?

They stood as I approached.

"I'd like to have a look at your things, in your dorm."

They looked at each other a bit fearfully, as if wondering amongst themselves as to whether I had the authority to make such a request. Boys need to know who the boss is, who's in charge, what the rules are, whether the rules be enforced fairly.

"Come on, let's go," I said, motioning for them to precede me, not allowing them any time to consider the question of who the boss was or whether I had the right to do what I was doing.

They took me to the main dormitory. On the ground floor was a large room, stuffed with bunk beds, where most of the boys resided. They each had one shelf of space to their name. I followed the boys through this room, ignoring the looks of several other boys already there, laying on their beds, or talking, as Bee, Yut, Nin and Cherd led to me their section of the dorm. They had two bunk-bed sets, side by side, and all their things rested on the shelves provided to them. They looked at me rather fearfully when I approached the shelves and began pawing through their stuff.

They had reason to.

Most of it was what you would expect to find among a teenage boy's possessions: Underwear, shorts, T-shirts, pencils, bus ticket stubs, and whatnot. But buried under a pile of clothes was a small brown bag, which could be tied at the top, similar to the one I had found in Brother Banditto's cell. I picked it up and undid the string, glancing over my shoulder at them in time to see their crestfallen faces.

Inside the bag were dozens of tablets and pills in small, wax-paper envelopes along with a mess of syringes, metal trays, lighters and packets of heroin.

Drugs.

"Would any of you care to explain?" I asked.

Three

I took the boys to the main office, and asked Kittisaro to summon Brother Khantiphalo. I expected Khantiphalo to be just as outraged as I was, but he was not. He looked through the bag I handed him, and then told his boys to go back to the dorm and wait for him there.

After they left, I was angry.

"You are going to punish them, aren't you?" I demanded.

Khantiphalo gave me an odd look, ignored my question, and asked Kittisaro whether the abbot was in his office.

Kittisaro nodded.

"We need to talk to the abbot."

We did?

I was quickly ushered into the abbot's office, and found myself sitting in the chair opposite the abbot's desk while Khantiphalo paced the floor behind me.

"Reverend Father, we need to tell him," Khantiphalo said to the abbot.

The abbot seemed to understand what this conveyed.

"Ananda, Brother Khantiphalo came to me this morning and told me about the conversation you'd had with him yesterday, about your having heard that drugs were being sold out of the temple. So I'm going to tell you what I told him, but aside from the three of us, no one else is to know what's really going on."

I sat back, frowning.

"The thing is, Ananda, I already know about these stories, and they're true. There is drug selling going on at this temple. But it's all a bit complicated, and I don't need some loose cannon shooting his mouth off to the wrong people. Am I making myself clear?"

I nodded.

"About a year ago, we took in four monks, who were supposedly transferring from a temple in Chiang Rai. I say supposedly because these men are not really monks. They are police officers. They're still police officers. They're working undercover, and they're trying to get to the bottom of the drug problem in this community — trying to figure out who's supplying the drugs, who's selling it, who's buying it, that sort of thing."

He folded his hands across his waist and gave me a long look.

I thought of the Gang of Three I had followed this morning — the very same ones whose files had "disappeared."

"And those monks wouldn't happen to be Satchapalo, Chutintharo, Panyathiro, and the missing Banditto?"

He sat forward abruptly in his seat. "How did you know that?

"I asked Kittisaro to figure who else's file we had misplaced, since we couldn't find Banditto's — that's how I know. I saw the three of them this morning going on an alms round together, and I thought it was too much of a coincidence, so I followed them."

I told him the whole story.

"So you would have figured it out sooner or later," he said with a smile.

I did not consider it amusing, and I was finding it hard to wrap my mind around the idea that the abbot had allowed four men to wear the robes for an entire year knowing they weren't monks, but rather police officers.

"Isn't there a law against a man wearing the robes who's not a monk?" I asked.

"That was my first question," the abbot said. "But I was assured that they had sought the proper permission."

"Assured by whom?"

"Well, they have to report to someone, don't they?"

"And does this someone have a name?"

The abbot looked uncomfortable.

"Does he?" I asked forcefully.

"His name is Pol Major General Chao –a big shot within the police department, from what I hear. He came and asked if I would allow him to carry out this operation at my temple. Offered to fund the-"

"-youth program," I answered.

He blinked.

"I got a call from him yesterday. Wanted to know how one of his boys came up dead."

"He's been using my boys as bait," Khantiphalo said angrily. "It's no skin off his nose if they come up murdered."

The abbot looked sheepish. "Well it's not as bad as all that," he said.

"It *is* as bad as all that," Khantiphalo said.

I had never seen him so angry.

"So you knew about the drugs these kids had?" I asked, turning to look at him.

"I thought all my kids were clean. I would never permit them to have drugs in the dorm or anywhere inside the monastery complex. I'm going to have to kick these kids out of my program now, and where are they going to go?"

Khantiphalo loved his kids, and was fiercely protective of them. I could see the thought of having to kick some of them out, and back onto the streets, was not sitting well with him at all.

"Maybe you can work out a deal with them?" I suggested.

He looked at me.

"We need to know if there are any monks involved," I said.

"That's for Chao and his men to figure out," the abbot interjected.

"We have monks at this temple selling drugs, and you're going to leave it to someone else to look into?" I asked.

"You don't know that for certain," he said defensively. "You don't know that any of our monks are involved."

That was true. We didn't. "But even if there's a possibility, we have to look into it. And you're the one authorized to do that, not Chao, no matter how high up the ladder he is."

"So what do you mean by a deal?" Khantiphalo asked.

"If they co-operate with us, you give them another chance. Let me interview them. I want to know where they got those drugs, and what they're doing with them — selling them? Using them? Delivering them to someone? If they don't want to co-operate, well, you'll have no choice but to expel them from the program."

"I'm all for it," Khantiphalo said, looking at the abbot.

The abbot regarded us both with what seemed to me an odd hesitation, as if he was weighing considerations in his mind that we knew nothing of — and would not likely approve.

"You know, Ananda," he said quietly, "by running off this boy Noot, you may have interfered in the work these undercover officers are trying to do — you may have run off the only contact they have with the bigger fish. If Chao gets wind of it, there could be hell to pay."

I didn't believe what I was hearing. "Who cares about Chao and his men?" I demanded. "Our duty and our responsibility lie with these boys, one of whom has managed to get himself whacked. Are you going to wait for a stack of dead bodies to pile up before you decide we need to take action?"

"I'm just trying to make you aware that the matter isn't quite as black and white as it might seem, Ananda," he said. "Chao is funding this program. If you spent have your time worrying about funding the way I do, you might see things a bit differently."

That was debatable, but he did have a point.

"Look," he said, setting forward in his chair, his fish eyes focuses on me intently. "Make your deal with these kids. Find out what you can. But do it discreetly. That's all I ask. It would be bad enough if word went around that our kids were doing drugs, much less our monks."

"The word's already going around," I pointed out.

"Rumors," the abbot said dismissively.

"I examined Brother Banditto's cell this morning," I said, taking another tack. "If I didn't know better, I would say he either ran off dressed in nothing but a sarong, or didn't run off at all."

"What do you mean?" the abbot asked.

"I mean both sets of his robes were in his cell. What did the man do – jump over the monastery wall at night in his sarong?"

"So what are you suggesting?"

"I'm suspicious, that's all. What have you been told about these police officers?"

The abbot shrugged. "I was told, in the beginning, that the operation wouldn't last more than three months. Now it's been a year. Now one of them has come up missing — Chao is convinced that his man didn't flee the scene, that something happened to him. But whether it's connected with Nong Noi's death or not, we don't know."

"You've been in touch with Chao? And you were going to tell me about this when, exactly?"

He again looked uncomfortable.

"How can I investigate the death of this boy if you're withholding information from me?" I asked. "I assumed Banditto was the killer, that he ran off after he committed the crime, that after a while we would be able to put the pieces together and figure out how he did it. Now you're telling me that it's not likely he was involved at all, that, in fact, he may have gotten himself in some sort of trouble. That means we must still have a killer on our hands, and I'm wasting my time chasing the wrong clues. That also means we need to be a lot more vigilant with these boys."

He grinned sheepishly.

"Is there anything else I should know?" I asked, feeling my old, impatient temper rising to the surface.

"Not at the moment," he said.

I stood, looked at Khantiphalo. "We've got some kids to interview, don't we?"

Four

Boys have a certain look to them when they know they've been busted, and I saw that look in each of the faces of the four boys waiting for us in the dorm.

I let Brother Khantiphalo address them first. He told them there was a serious problem at hand, that he might consider working out a deal with them if they would co-operate and let us know where the drugs had come from and what they were doing with them, or planning to do with them.

As he spoke, I watched the boys' faces. A couple of those faces were hard, cynical, but the other two seemed hopeful — the prospect of a deal put a little bit of strength back into their limbs.

"Noot isn't coming back," I said, just in case they thought there might be a price to pay for the information they provided. "If he returns, we'll just keep throwing him out until he gets the message."

The boys looked at each other, having secret conversations with their eyes and body language.

"And you'll let us stay?" Bee asked. He was the youngest, maybe all of fourteen or fifteen, and would find it the most frightening to be kicked out and put back on the street — or worse. He had the sort of delicate-boned body and hesitant demeanor that I associated with kids who often got picked on.

"Don't say a word," Yut said, giving him an angry glare. Yut was tall, muscular, handsome, and hard-faced.

The other two boys, Nin and Cherd, were obviously followers, and would follow whoever won this argument.

I decided to intervene with a bit of a scare tactic. "Maybe we didn't make it clear what we meant by expelling you from the program. Just in case you're not sure, that means turning you over to the police, who will remand you to the juvenile division where you will be placed in detention until you're eighteen years old. Since you will have been caught possessing drugs, when you are released you will be on probation and any further offences will get you sent to Klong Prem."

Klong Prem was the prison situated in the heart of Bangkok, and if there was one place in this city you didn't want to go, this was the most likely candidate.

My words had the desired effect. Bee wouldn't look at Yut. The two followers were now nervous, hesitant, not at all in a hurry to be remanded over to the authorities.

"Fuck this," Yut said. He grabbed up his things. "You aint sending me to no fucking juvenile center. You'll have to kill me first."

He stuffed his things in his backpack, glaring at us to see if would dare try to stop him. Khantiphalo was going to do just that, but I put a hand on his arm and restrained him. It was better to let one go, if we could help the others, and Yut clearly wasn't about to tell us anything.

"Ain't you gonna stop me, holy man?" Yut asked defiantly, sneering at me.

I stared at him for a long moment, to let him know his show of bravura wasn't really working. "Don't ever come here again," I said quietly.

"Yeah, well, fuck you," he said, stalking off through the dorm.

"Now," I said to Bee, Nin and Cherd after Yut had left. "Would any of you like to tell me what's going on?"

They did.

They were, as it turned out, working for Noot, making small deliveries in exchange for small sums of cash. They knew it was wrong, but they needed the money. Bee, at least, had been sick to death they would be found out and expelled, and said he was glad that we knew, and that he had been too afraid of Yut to tell Khantiphalo or anyone else.

No matter how I pressed them, they simply didn't know for whom Noot was working, although they admitted they had seen him often talking to Banditto and Satchapalo. Noot had told them Banditto was his uncle, so they had thought nothing of it.

By the time I was finished, Khantiphalo was just getting ready to start, and I suspected his concerns were rather different than mine — but at least his kids wouldn't be expelled, and I could see the gratitude in his eyes.

Five

I went to my kuti and sat down on the porch, cross-legged. I needed to spend some time meditating, being quiet, giving my mind a chance to relax, but also to put together some of the pieces of what I'd learned in the past few days. I couldn't force myself to figure things out, but if I was patient, if I let my mind have a bit of room to maneuver, it would begin suggesting solutions on its own.

I did some breathing exercises, trying to let the tension out of my body, trying to relax and let go, in the way Brother Thammarato had taught me.

For perhaps thirty minutes, I did nothing but sit there, enjoying it, not allowing myself to be rushed, not allowing my head to be filled with desperate thoughts.

The sky, I noticed, was overcast. The air was becoming muggy and unbearable again. I hoped the rains would begin soon. I longed for the sound of the large drops splashing on the ground, crashing against the roofs of the kutis, soaking everything and forming small pools and ponds on the grounds among the trees. I longed for the way the air would turn cool just before the rains began, the way the breeze would blow up, driving away the mosquitoes. I longed for the way that everything seemed cleaner afterwards, the air having lost its heaviness, the sky returning to blue.

I began to run all the events over in my mind, comparing them to what I now knew about Satchapalo and the others — that there was an undercover operation going on in our monastery. But nothing added up properly. If Banditto wasn't the killer, and if Satchapalo was not a suspect, then I was left with Brother Chittakhutto, our budding Buddhist scholar that Nong Noi had been visiting at night, and I knew he wasn't the one who had killed Nong Noi.

I was left with nothing.

There was someone, I thought, who would be good to talk to at this point — my old captain at the police station, Khun Charn. I had served under him for almost ten years. Whenever I had a complicated case, I would sit in his office and go through it, piece by piece, getting his read, his thoughts, his take. He was one of the best minds around in the old days, and I had learned much from him.

I'd not gone to see him for years now.

I collected my things and put on my traveling shoes.

At the main office, I asked Kittisaro to summon Jak for me, so he could get some money from the treasurer and accompany me.

While waiting, a thought had occurred to me that I wanted to take up with Kittisaro.

"Do you get on the Internet?" I asked. "With all your computers and stuff?"

"Oh, Ananda, please," he said dismissively. "This isn't the Stone Age."

I was now going to try to have a technical conversation about something that was completely beyond me. I understood that one could "go on the Internet" to find information.

"I was wondering," I said, "if you went on the Internet, could you find information about gouged out eyes. Would that be possible?"

"Gouged out eyes?"

I nodded.

"In what context?" he asked.

"In the context of having a dead boy in one of our bathrooms with gouged out eyes. In other words, has it happened before? Is there anything significant about it? Why would you gouge out someone's eyes? That sort of thing."

"I can look, and see what's there. Do you mean something like news reports of other crimes where the victims had their eyes taken out?"

"Exactly. Do you have access to news reports?"

"Ananda, most newspapers have their entire archives online these days. You can look up any story you want. You can run searches, query their databases, look for keywords. It's amazing. What century are you living in?"

"Query something and see what you can find."

"Not a problem," he said.

His comment about archives got me to thinking. "Can you find out anything about someone named Chao, a police major general?"

"Should I give you a piece of paper and you can make a list?" he asked.

Six

I stood at Khun Charn's door, filled with trepidation. Visiting your past was not always a good idea.

"Aren't you going to ring the bell?" Jak asked, annoyed.

I reached up and pushed the button before my hand could decide otherwise.

A young woman — Charn's daughter, if I remembered correctly — came to the door and gave me a confused look.

"Is your father home?" I asked. "If it's not a good time, I could come back later."

"I'll get him," she said.

About a minute later, an old man appeared, walking slowly toward the door.

I greeted him, offering him a respectful wai.

"Ananda? Is that you?"

I nodded.

His face broke into a broad smile. "Come in, Ananda, please. And I see you've brought a friend."

I introduced Jak.

"Your kuti boy?" the old man asked.

I glanced at Jak, saw something in his eyes there that made me say, "Yes. He is."

"Well, come in, both of you.

We were seated in the living room. Charn was an avid reader, and so too, I discovered, was my would-be kuti boy.

Jak wandered up and down the many bookcases in Charn's house, his eyes large with amazement.

"Help yourself," Charn called. "A boy who reads! That's a boy who goes places!"

Jak settled himself somewhere on the floor, looking at old novels.

Charn's daughter brought drinks, putting them on the coffee table before us.

We talked quietly.

"What brings you here?" Charn asked, giving me a kindly look. "Not that I'm not glad to see you. But after what happened ... well, you just sort of disappeared."

I nodded. I had, indeed. I had disappeared quite completely into the orange robes.

"I'm investigating a murder," I said. "And I thought maybe you could help me figure it out. I've got a lot of pieces, but I just can't make sense of them. And this whole business — one of the boys at our temple came up dead a few days ago — has reminded me of things, and I suddenly thought I should come see you. It's been too long."

"So what do you have?" he asked, in the same tone of voice that he'd asked that question many times before. And like I'd done many times before, I laid the case out, piece by piece, telling him everything.

I pictured the dead boy in my mind, lying on the floor of the bathroom with his gouged out eyes and cigarette burns, the candle stuffed in his mouth.

When I had finished speaking, I settled back in my chair.

"It's all very suggestive, isn't it?" Charn said.

"But I'm interested in your take on the situation."

He sat back in his chair, put his hands behind his head. His legendary brain went to work.

"The candle in the mouth," he said quietly, eyes closed, lost in thought. "Suggests silencing, doesn't it? A sort of shut up or else. A bit of overkill. Or maybe it was put there to confuse us as to the cause of death. Was he choked? Did he drown? Or did he die in some other fashion, and the candle was put there to throw us off the scent? From what you've said, it doesn't appear the boy drowned. He could have, mind you — someone could have dunked his head in that water jar and kept it there until the boy stopped moving. But you saw no evidence of that. So how did he really die?"

He was silent for a long moment.

"The whole thing seems angry, doesn't it? If you were just going to kill the boy, why not do it? Why the cigarette burns? Was he tortured? Was someone trying to find out whether he did something, said something, spilled the beans? From what you tell me about this reporter, it seems clear he was trying to do just that, but she didn't believe him. So maybe he was trying to gather some evidence, got himself caught. Maybe he was tortured because the killer wanted to know what he had said, who he had said it to, if he had said anything at all.

"But in general, this seems like a crime of passion. The eyes — why would you do that to someone? Again, it's suggestive — it's like the boy saw something, and the killer was punishing him, making sure he would never see anything else. It's disfiguring, isn't it? Was he a good-looking kid?"

I had to think about that. I suppose he was, and I said so.

Charn opened his eyes and sat forward, regarding me intently. "This was an angry act, an angry crime, something personal. Why would you be angry with a homeless boy living at a temple, unless he stumbled onto something — and if he did, just whack him. Why the overkill? If he was good looking, maybe the point was to disfigure him. The eyes are accusing, aren't they? So you take them out to stop the accusations. And from what you've told of the boy, his behavior, his going to the kutis of the monks at night — it suggests he made someone really angry. Maybe he kept pestering that person until he got himself killed. Maybe it was all done in a rage, on the spur of the moment, and the killer tried to disguise the killing, or confuse it, by dumping the boy in the water."

He shook his head. "Poor boy."

I sighed, feeling exactly the same way.

"So," he said, "what's your read?"

It was my turn to participate in this ritual.

"If it was suicide, where are the boy's eyes? If you can gouge your own eyes out — if that's even possible — then your hands would be bloody, wouldn't they? And although his hands were in the water, I didn't see any traces of blood on them. So that rules out his death being self-afflicted.

"The candle in the mouth — I thought maybe he was choked to death with it. Or maybe it was to just punish or humiliate him."

"Exactly!" Charn exclaimed, sitting forward and slapping his knee. "And why would you want to do that, unless you were really angry with the boy about something? Was he involved with someone? A lover's spat? It happens at monasteries, from what I hear."

It did happen.

"But there are some things bothering me," I said. "I looked around for footprints in the area of the bathroom. From there to the back wall, there's nothing but dirt and sand, no grass, a few leaves but not many. If someone had brought the body over the wall and placed it in the bathroom, they would have left footprints."

"So it was an inside job."

"Yes," I said. "It would have to be. Someone had to take the body through the monastery complex itself, to get to that bathroom. On the other hand, the crime might have been committed in the bathroom itself and the boy went there willingly with the killer. But I don't buy that because although I found Nong Noi's shirt and shorts, I did not find any shoes, and his feet were far too clean for him to have been walking around the grounds bare-footed. It seems far more likely that he was killed somewhere else, and then carried to the bathroom."

"But why arrange the body the way it was? Why put him in the water?"

I bit at my lower lip. I didn't know.

"You said rigor mortis had already passed?" he asked.

"And it also occurred to me that, in order for his body to have been found in the state it was, he had to have been taken to the bathroom just after the murder. If rigor mortis had set in, his body would not have fit so well into the water jar. It would have been stiff and unyielding."

One point was particularly bothering me. "His body must have been in the bathroom all day long, and no one noticed," I said. Since that bathroom was only about a hundred meters down from my own kuti, it disturbed me that a dead body could be so close at hand without my being aware of it.

"If the door was closed, who would know? But eventually it would start to smell," Charn said.

Was the door closed? The abbot said he thought someone was sleeping inside, and so paused to have a look. So the door must have been open.

"What if the door wasn't closed?" I asked.

He offered a smile — not that the subject was humorous, but to suggest I was on to something.

"The temple dogs!" I exclaimed. "If the door had been open, the dogs would have smelled the body and begun to congregate around the bathroom. Someone would have noticed. *I* would have noticed."

Charn nodded. He could see the point exactly without my having to explain. "But then someone must have opened the door. The abbot?"

We both considered this for a long while in silence.

For just a moment, I was missing the old days, missing the banter, the tossing around of clues and ideas, picking the collective mind, as it were, trying to reason through the chaos to find a solution.

For just a moment.

"Maybe there's something the abbot isn't telling you," Charn suggested. "Or maybe the killer wanted the body to be found, but was afraid no one was going to if the door remained shut, so he went back and opened it."

Why would the killer want the body to be found? The more time that went by, the more the body decayed and the trail grew colder.

"And what about motive?" Charn asked. "If you've got a dead body, then you've got someone hanging around who had enough reason to kill. Who would have wanted to kill this boy?"

I gave this a fair amount of thought — we both did.

The picture that was emerging of Nong Noi was that of someone who was not well liked, someone with emotional problems, who irritated others. But was that enough for someone to kill him? Were his visits to the kutis at night — to Chittakhutto and Satchapalo, and perhaps others — enough to incite a murderous rage?

On the other hand, if he had been involved with one of the monks — if he'd been having a sexual relationship — and if that relationship went sour, or if Nong Noi refused to end it, a crime of passion might well have ensued.

I suggested this to Charn, and he nodded.

"Murder is often about love gone bad," he said softly. "If the other person can't accept your decision to leave, to call it quits, if passions are high, if the heart is involved — yes, that would explain the anger that seems apparent in this boy's death. Maybe he spurned someone. Or maybe he pushed someone too far. Or maybe he was blackmailing someone."

I thought of Brother Satchapalo. It was not hard for me to imagine him killing a boy such as Noi, disgusted by his behavior, especially if the boy had come on to him in a sexual manner. A man could get violently angry about such a thing.

There was another matter I wanted to ask Charn about.

"What do you know about someone named Police Major General Chao, a big shot at the police department headquarters?"

Charn's eyebrows went up. "Chao? Clean as a whistle, from what I've heard. Why do you ask?"

I explained about Chao and his funding of our youth program, and his undercover operation. I was suspicious, basically. The idea of putting anti-narcotics agents under cover in a Buddhist monastery was preposterous.

Charn agreed. "That is a bit dodgy. Also against the law. I'm not sure any exception would be made, for whatever reason — you can't have Buddhist monks walking around, participating in ceremonies, funerals, blessing houses, whatever, while they're not really monks. The lay people would be scandalized. They would be furious. I can't see any situation where that would be allowed."

My thoughts exactly.

"But Chao," he added, "seems above board. He was appointed a few years when the new government took office and wanted to improve the image of the police department among the people. Chao was educated in the US, from what I understand, even did an interview with CNN once, perfect English — you would have thought he grew up in California or something. Got an advanced degree in forensic science, really knows his stuff. Still goes out on the beat, they say, and helps his detectives solve the more difficult crimes. I've never heard a bad word said about the man. In fact, some of the guys under him transferred out because they like doing things the old way — getting kickbacks and all that — and he wouldn't have any of it. And some younger guys today actually ask to be put under him, because they believe in him, and want to clean up the police force, get the police back on the side of the law."

I offered him a small frown. And yet, it made perfect sense: The most notorious criminals in our society had very pleasing public faces indeed, and got away with all sorts of things. Just about every politician had bank accounts stuffed with cash from bribes, double-dealing, influence peddling, and the like. The sons of one famous and wealthy politician were notoriously rowdy: One tried to run over a police officer with his car, another was accused of shooting a police officer dead during a late night scuffle at a nightclub, and yet they got away with their crimes, time and again, because their father was rich and his family was untouchable, no matter what they did. Witnesses were intimidated or paid off, evidence was lost, a corrupt court dismissed the cases — with enough money to grease the wheels, anything was possible.

So it would come as no surprise if Chao were just the opposite of what he appeared to be in public.

And yet, most of those returning from overseas with advanced degrees were on fire with the desire to bring our country up to date, to stamp out corruption, to have transparent government, to put an end to the inept justice system, to ensure fairness for all citizens, regardless of economic status or background. Sometimes we laughed at them, but in a self-conscious way, because they put truths on the table that we weren't always comfortable looking at. We wanted to believe that we were just as good as the Americans or the Brits, but we knew we were not, and no one would ever dare say so publicly because we were all in a collective denial of the truth.

So maybe Chao was legitimate. Maybe he had somehow obtained permission to put agents undercover at a monastery.

"If it's not a legitimate operation," I asked, "then what would be the point? Why would he have four men taking the robes and staying at a monastery?"

"Would be the perfect place to hide out from the law, wouldn't it?"

"Hide out?"

"It's been done before, Ananda. A man's wanted by the law, runs off to a Buddhist monastery, gets himself admitted as a monk. The law can't touch him until he's defrocked or exposed. Pretty soon, the heat dies down, and he goes on about his business, and no one's ever the wiser."

I gave this a long moment of thought.

"What if," I said, a bit excitedly, "there is indeed a drug problem at my temple — and these men are involved somehow? When I followed them yesterday, they went to a private residence. Are they picking up their supplies there? Making deliveries?"

I remembered what the reporter at Thai Rath had said concerning her conversation with Nong Noi, that there were monks getting the boys to make deliveries. There had to be something to deliver. But the monks weren't cooking up ecstasy and heroin in their kutis, were they?

After Charn listened to my retelling of that conversation with the reporter, he raised his eyebrows, his eyes twinkling. "Maybe that's your answer," he said. "Maybe your boy got himself killed because he got himself messed up with those monks. Didn't you say he was visiting one of their kutis?"

"Brother Satchapalo's. If Noi was making deliveries for them — and he told the reporter he was — then maybe Satchapalo isn't telling me everything about what went on between them."

"And yet you have to be careful," Charn said, offering me a word of warning. "It could be that those men are police officers after all. Somehow you'll have to find out."

The conversation lulled, and I was afraid I might be taxing Charn's health.

He sat forward. "Ananda, it's like I've told you many times. Follow the leads. Follow the leads. The rest of it is distraction."

I smiled. I had forgotten that. But that bit of advice had come in handy on numerous occasions.

"How are the years treating you, Ananda?" Charn asked.

I didn't know how to answer that question.

"There are good days and bad days," I said quietly.

Seven

Jak and I returned to the monastery in time for the 4 p.m. funeral chants for Nong Noi.

We assembled in the largest funeral hall that the monastery complex had, and Nong Noi himself was inside a cheap wooden coffin, propped up on wooden sawhorses, up in the front, with but one flower arrangement placed on top of the coffin. It was the arrangement that I had asked Jak to go across the main road and purchase at the florist shop.

I had some money to my name – not much, but some. Whenever a person died, it was customary to ask monks to offer chants, and the monks were offered a small token of appreciation in the form of bank notes. These funds were collected by the treasurer and kept in our accounts, and from time to time we were allowed to purchase things, but only with the abbot's permission.

So I had spent some of my "money" because when I arrived yesterday for the chants and saw the coffin sitting there, alone, without decoration, without any flowers to show that someone cared, that someone remembered, I couldn't bear it.

This was the second day of funeral chants that we would offer. Tomorrow would be the last. Tomorrow Nong Noi would be cremated.

I looked around, wondering if Jut, Noi's cousin, would come. Aside from the monks and dek wats, there was no one else in attendance.

I remembered what Jut said about Noi's mother hanging herself, and I felt a small wave of grief. AIDS was ravaging the north of Thailand — we all knew that. We knew the statistics. We read the reports. More than a few innocent women had philandering husbands who contracted the disease and then came home and gave it to their wives. The statistic we called "AIDS orphans" was composed of children left behind after both parents had died of the disease. That statistic kept rising.

Nong Noi had been one of those kids. How many others were there?

I tried to concentrate on the death chants, recalling what the Lord Buddha had often said: Everything is impermanent. Nothing lasts forever. Nothing — and no one.

CHAPTER FOUR

"The fool thinks an evil deed as sweet as honey, so long as it does not ripen (does not produce results). When it ripens, the fool comes to grief."

The Lord Buddha. From the Dhammapada #69.

ONE

The next day was Saturday, and I remembered Lt. Somchai's invitation for Jak to play football on Saturday mornings at the police department field, and I reminded Jak of this after breakfast. I also wanted to check in with Somchai and see if he'd made any progress.

Jak gave me a shy smile, said nothing.

"You don't want to go?" I asked.

"They'll make fun of me," he said, not giving me his eyes.

"Why would they do that?" I asked.

"You know," he said.

His leg.

"Who cares if they make fun?" I asked. "You'll enjoy yourself, and that's what matters. You can show them a thing or two."

His face brightened. "You think so?"

"I know so," I said.

He did not want to go — and yet he did. Was I wrong to nurse his hopes that he could play together with other kids, and not be mercilessly teased, excluded, laughed at? Maybe this time it would be different. Maybe there would be other kids with disabilities, and he wouldn't feel so alone.

We were soon ensconced on the monk's seat in a dingy bus, on our way to the station, the passengers around me no doubt hating my guts and whispering "Yellow Tiger" behind my back.

Saturday morning traffic was particularly gruesome — it seemed anyone who had any business to attend to did it on a Saturday morning. Stops at traffic lights lasted up to ten minutes. We surged ahead a few bus-lengths and then stopped. A lorry stalled out in the lane ahead of us, backing up traffic and causing even more chaos. Pedestrians were out in force. Motorcyclists weaved through the traffic at death-defying speeds. The bus itself was jammed with so many bodies it was hard to breathe. It certainly provided a great many opportunities to practice the virtues of detachment and long-suffering.

We arrived at out stop at last, and pushed our way through the sea of bodies and out of the bus doors.

Kids had already gathered at the police station, hanging out on the steps, and as we approached, Jak hid behind me as he always did, nervous and uncertain of himself.

"Are you here to play football?" I asked, standing in the midst of the kids.

They laughed, happy and excited, some nodding their heads.

"Are you the captain?" one asked. "Are you going to play?"

I laughed myself, and shook my head. "But I have a friend who would like to play. His name is Jak. I've been told he can kick that ball like nobody's business."

I encouraged Jak to show himself.

"Is that true?" one of the boys asked, eyes wide.

Kids will believe anything.

Jak looked at me, sheepish and uncertain.

"Of course it is," I said, "and I hope you don't find out the hard way."

They started introducing themselves and they were soon carrying on as if they'd known each other all their lives, in that way that kids do.

A young officer came down the steps of the station, carrying jerseys — half of them green, the other half red. He greeted me with a smile, and I introduced him to Jak. A number of "new" kids had shown up, so Jak was not alone. Most of these kids were inner-city youths, from poor families, no doubt just as embarrassed about their poverty as Jak was about his leg.

The officer handed out the jerseys. It was to be reds against greens that day. He led them off to the nearby park, and I watched Jak following along, hoping he would have some fun.

I went inside, wondering if Lt. Somchai would be around so I could talk to him.

As luck would have it, he was.

"You guys still work Saturday mornings?" I asked, giving him a grin. Most officers put in a full five days of work, and then another half-day, either on Saturday or Sunday. Or at least they did in the old days.

"Gives me something to do," he said, showing me a bit of his black humor. "I've been meaning to get over your way and update you."

We sat down at his desk. I was all ears.

"Couldn't do much with the business card and newspaper you gave me," he said, retrieving an envelope with the card and medal in it. "But the medal was another story."

He took the medal out and slid it across the table. "My wife figured it out, actually. Put some of her magazines to use for a change. You know she collects those magazines — they have all the details about these medals, how many were made, who made them, who owns them, what the going rate is, all of that stuff. Well, she finally tracked this down to a temple in Ubon Ratchathani, a village called Tan Sum. It's fairly old, too. It was made about ten years ago, by the abbot at the village temple there. He was pretty famous in his day, from what I hear. After he died, his medals became quite valuable as collector's items. My wife says this one ought to fetch you a pretty penny, if you were to sell it. But given that it is evidence in a murder investigation, there's not much chance of that."

I looked at the medal. It had a Buddha image engraved on the front, an ornate triangle representing a temple on the back.

Ubon Ratchathani.

Why did that name ring a bell?

"Do you know anyone from there?" he asked, guessing at my thoughts.

"It seems I do," I said. "But it's not coming to me just yet."

"Where was the boy from?" he asked.

"Chiang Mai."

"So he was either given the medal, or the killer dropped it when he dumped the body?"

I nodded. But since the boy didn't have a chain around his neck — most devotees of medals wear a chain full of medals that hang around their necks and clank together all the time — and since the boy was most likely dead when he was taken to the bathroom, I was willing to gamble that the medal belonged to the killer.

Ubon Ratchathani. I remembered seeing that name recently. But where?

"Aside from that," Somchai said, "I'm afraid I can't help you."

Somchai accompanied me out of the station and even walked with me to park nearby.

The kids were engrossed in their game of soccer. Jak wore a red jersey and manned the far net, smiling. With his leg, he wasn't much good running around the field, but as a goalie he kept his eyes on the ball and when it started making its way down the field toward him, he was on it in a flash, throwing himself at that ball as if his life depended on it.

The reds appeared to be winning. The greens couldn't, no matter how they tried, get a ball past Jak and into the net, and I could see him grinning with mad pleasure each time he blocked an attack and had the chance to toss the ball back into play.

It made me think life wasn't so bad after all.

Two

At 4 p.m. we gathered to offer the last of our funeral chants for Nong Noi. All the monks and most of the boys were present, but the abbot was strangely absent, and Thammarato had been called upon to lead the chants.

I couldn't keep my mind on the ancient Pali words today. There were 200 standard chants, all in Pali, and I had memorized about a third of them. Most monks need about twenty years in the monastery before they become proficient, and I had a long way to go.

For the second time in recent memory, I was going to break with convention and do something I was not supposed to do. I stood up, and respectfully, slowly, walked back through the ranks of monks and boys to the rear of the prayer hall, pausing to survey the whole scene.

There were looks, of course — a monk was never supposed to get up and leave a chanting session. But I wanted to see who was there, and who, perhaps, was not. It was bothering me that the abbot was absent when he had made such a display of making certain the rest of us would not be.

The monks were lined up properly, the older ones in front, the younger in back, moving from most senior to most novice — our latest arrived not more than two weeks ago — with the temple boys and other boys sitting in the very back, doing their best to look attentive and prayerful although they couldn't understand the words to the chants, and couldn't follow along or participate.

I looked for Jut, but she had not come, and probably would not.

I left the prayer hall and walked around it, slowly, the late afternoon sun hot on the back of my neck, the temple dogs slumbering in whatever shady, out-of-the-way spots they could find. In the parking lot I saw a car with the Thai Rath logo emblazoned on the side, the boot open, a photographer digging through his camera equipment, getting ready to take pictures of the cremation. Yesterday's edition had featured the naked Nong Noi (a tiny strip of black covering his privates) on the front page. This was next to the picture of a beautiful, half-naked actress who wittered on about the glories of plastic surgery — see inside for the full story.

No one else was about in the parking lot, and I walked slowly up to the main dormitory and then inside. This building had five stories, and close to 200 rooms, each smaller than the last, some of them more like closets than a monk's cell.

It was silent.

A long hallway led through the middle of it, giving way on the far side to another entrance. I walked down the length of it. If Nong Noi had been killed inside this building, how would he have been carried through this building and outside without anyone noticing? Who would have the nerve to risk such a thing? Even in the dead of night, you could not be certain that someone, somewhere, was not awake — on their way to the toilet, unable to sleep, sick, any number of things.

I went out the far end and found myself staring at the temple, which was blocked off by a low iron fence with a small gate, designed to keep dogs and other animals away. I undid the latch on the gate and went inside, removing my shoes on the steps to the temple and going inside bare-footed. An enormous Buddha sat inside, in a cross-legged meditation position, his hands folded together on his lap — the Thursday position, as it was known. There were seven standard Buddha poses, each known by a day of the week, and we had smaller statues of these sitting in front of the main image.

My favorite was the Tuesday Buddha, with the Buddha lying down, symbolizing his achievement of Nirvana — a well-deserved rest after a long struggle. Somehow or other, that seemed appropriate for me, a worthwhile goal.

In front of our Thursday Buddha were numerous candles, the short, fat ones in front, the tall ones behind. They were all lit, casting flickering shadows about the wall, and rays of light on the Buddha figure. There was also a large monk's bowl there for the faithful to put one-baht coins in, which they believed would bring good luck.

I went up to the Buddha and stared at him for a long time, wondering how he had ever managed to cease craving things when it seemed like all I ever did was crave things. I looked again at the candles, remembering the one stuffed in Nong Noi's mouth. Where had the killer gotten it? Here? I looked at the candles, but none were missing. Where else could they be gotten?

I went outside, back into the glare of the sun, and continued walking. Something was wrong somewhere — I could sense it. I was not the superstitious sort, but very often, in my police work, I had gut feelings about things, intuitions. It was as if my brain was trying to get me to wake up to some important fact, to something I had overlooked, as if it had already figured things out and was trying to find a way to let me know.

So I trusted my instincts, and many times had been proved right.

My instincts, at this moment, were telling me something was amiss.

But, what?

I continued walking. Temple complexes were not generally well organized or laid out in a predetermined, orderly fashion. Buildings were added as need and finances allowed, put wherever there was a spot, without anyone ever giving the matter much thought. Wat Mahanat was no different. The main dorm and the large sala were out in front, with the huge crematorium, an obelisk-like structure that rose about twenty meters into the air. Next came the temple, in the center, with more funeral halls, or small salas, on one side, and the monk's prayer hall on the other. Passing by them, one entered the grounds where the first thing to be encountered was the large office and the monk's dining hall and laundry, and then a stone's throw away from that, the abbot's kuti, which in this case was rather too large to be called a kuti. After that, the small huts, or monks' kutis, were visible, stretching away into the distance, hidden by trees and large plants, with the occasional odd bathroom built here and there, again as time and need dictated. In the center of all that was our bo tree.

In other words, if Nong Noi had been killed in the main dormitory, his body would have to have been carried from there (down who knows how many flights of stairs and past numerous cells), past the temple and funeral halls, past the abbot's quarters and the main office and the dining room, and then through the maze of kutis, all the way to the back where that last, final bathroom had been built.

That pretty much argued against Nong Noi having been killed in the dorm. But if not there, then where? The dormitory cells were the only places — with the exception of the kutis — that offered some privacy, where a monk could close the door and expect not to be disturbed, and if you were torturing and murdering someone, you would not want to be disturbed.

I walked past the main office and the abbot's kuti and continued on. The largest bathroom was there, just past the abbot's quarters, and I heard water splashing.

Someone was taking a shower, dousing himself with bowls of water.

Curious, I walked up to the bathroom and paused, listening. I peered around the corner at the entrance, surprised to see the abbot himself dousing his body with water, his bald head soapy with shampoo, soap bubbles all over the floor. I was even more surprised to see his monk's robes on the floor, sopping wet, as if he had been or was planning to wash them by hand.

Feeling rather guilty, I retreated. The abbot had to shower and wash his robes sometime, didn't he? And perhaps he had simply lost track of the time.

I began walking from one kuti to the next, realizing that Nong Noi must have been killed in one of them. But which one? Of the twenty-five monks or so that occupied them, I could safely cross most off the list. I had known too many of them for too long to believe them capable of murder. Still, I examined each one of them, even poking my nose in the doors and looking around. But this turned up nothing.

My footsteps took me back to the funeral hall, where I resumed my seat, ignoring the disapproving looks around me.

The chants ended, and Nong Noi's coffin was taken down from the saw-horses on which it had sat for the past three days. With the coffin being carried by some of the younger monks, we processed around the crematorium three times, and then watched as the coffin was carried up the crematorium steps and placed on more saw-horses, awaiting the last ritual before both coffin and body would be cremated.

There was some uncertainty about what would happen next, because normally this was the time when the relatives took one last look at their loved one — the lid to the coffin, which had been nailed shut, was pried up while the loved ones gathered around. A coconut was broken over the deceased's head, the water inside it spilled over the head and face. If there were any personal items or articles of clothing that the relatives wished to have cremated along with the body, they were placed inside the coffin during this time.

Given what had happened to Nong Noi, there was doubt about whether this bit of the ritual would be carried out. I was not there when the body had been prepared for burial, so did not know if Nong Noi had been completely wrapped in a sheet, hiding his face, or not.

Three

The abbot appeared at the crematorium and went to the top of the stairs alone. He stood by the coffin for several moments, head bowed. Despite his large size, he now seemed rather small and forlorn, and I suppose he was feeling just as lousy about this whole affair as the rest of us were. The death of any child is a sad occasion, but worse when it happens on your watch, when it is your responsibility to protect that child, and you fail.

Brother Suchinno went up the stairs next, carrying the small crowbar used to pry lids off coffins. The abbot turned to us, waiting below.

"Will the senior monks come up please? And Nong Noi's friends, too. The rest of you, please wait."

Along with the senior monks, I went up the stairs, followed by a few boys who seemed nervous and out of sorts. One of those boys, I saw with a start, was Bee. His large eyes seemed lost and frightened. I didn't know he had been a friend of Noi's, hadn't thought to ask.

Brother Suchinno worked to pry open the coffin lid.

Bee looked up at me and seemed uncertain, as if looking for a friendly face in the crowd. I nodded to him and motioned for him to stand beside me. He needed no further prompting.

"Are you alright?" I asked, taking his hand.

He looked up at me, but didn't answer. He seemed painfully frail today, his shoulders too thin, no courage in his limbs. He rested his face against my shoulder as if he thought I would protect him from something.

The lid eventually came up.

The abbot handed Brother Suchinno a coconut. With a large knife that he kept stashed somewhere in his robes, he split the coconut, first hefting it up into the air and whacking it expertly with the knife, somehow managing to do all of that and then catching the coconut, without letting the knife fly off and maim someone.

I moved closer and peered inside the coffin. Nong Noi had been wrapped in a sheet, and there was nothing to see of him. The coconut water was spilled over his face.

We did our best to follow all the proper rituals, believing that Nong Noi's spirit would be assisted by our help. For three days we had brought food and water to the funeral hall to offer to Nong Noi, in case he case he needed them. We offered chants to show him that we had remembered him. We burned incense to demonstrate the sacredness of his death, hoping the sweet smell of it would carry him up and onto whatever his next life might be. Now we were going to burn his body so that he wouldn't continue to return to it.

That he had died violently was all the more reason to carry out these rituals — it was believed that ghosts and spirits were those who had died violently and had not been helped to make their passage to another life, and thus were angry with those they had left behind and sought to punish them.

I didn't always believe such things myself, but I was decidedly in the minority.

One of the younger monks offered each of us a small flower made of sandalwood, which we put into the coffin. The more morbid part of my mind was reminded me that these flowers were to help make certain the body caught fire once the crematorium was turned on.

I placed my flower in the coffin. Bee, holding on to my arm — squeezing it rather too tightly — peered from around my shoulder at his friend and burst into tears. I turned to comfort him, but he pulled away, and pointed at the body.

"That's not Noi," he whispered, looking into my eyes. He was sniffling and miserable, but seemed absolutely sure of himself.

I turned to look at the sheet-wrapped body. If it wasn't Nong Noi, who was it? And how could it be anyone else but Noi?

I turned and tried to motion Bee away. Perhaps the day's activities were getting to him. He appeared to be no more than fourteen, and kids were not exactly good with death and sometimes did strange things in the face of it.

"No!" he exclaimed, pulling free of my grasp. "That's not Noi," he said loudly.

We were all stopped in our tracks. The senior monks looked at Bee as if he'd lost his mind.

"It isn't!" he insisted. "Noi was a lot thinner. I'm not lying!"

I looked again at the sheet-wrapped body and frowned. The boy had a point. The body I had found dumped in the bathroom had been painfully thin. This body had a full chest and wide hips.

"Ananda!" the abbot exclaimed. "Get this boy out of here."

The abbot was now in our faces, shooing us both away, his eyes popping out of their sockets.

"The boy's right," I said.

"That's idiotic," the abbot replied under his breath.

"It wouldn't hurt to check," I said quietly. "I'll do it."

The abbot cursed — rather out of character for him — and then said, "Don't make a show of it. There's damned photographers out there from Thai Rath. Okay? I've had enough of this nonsense."

I felt sorry for him. I'd had quite enough myself. But it wouldn't hurt to check and see, just to be certain. And I had a sneaking suspicion that I knew exactly whose body was in that coffin.

I went to the coffin and positioned myself next to the head. The sheet had been wrapped over the head and down the shoulders, and I couldn't get to the face without undoing half of it. Brother Suchinno stood next to me, a baffled look on his face.

"Where's your knife?" I asked quietly.

He handed over his big butcher knife, and I cut a small slit in the fabric of the sheet over Noi's face and peered through it.

Bee was right.

This was not Nong Noi.

Four

"You're out of your mind!" the abbot exclaimed loudly.

I didn't respond.

"It can't be," he said, huffing and puffing and angry and wringing his hands together, desperate to not accept the truth. "This is outrageous!"

"Well, whatever *this* is," I said evenly, "it's not Nong Noi in that coffin and you have to call this cremation off."

"But the reporters!"

"To hell with them," I said. "You can't cremate someone and not even know who it is. Don't be stupid. And besides, we both know who that is."

"We do?" he said, astonished.

"Of course we do."

The senior monks had stepped back, aware that something was seriously wrong. Brother Suchinno had cut the fabric even further, and now there was a gasp as the senior monks came forward and discovered that Nong Noi was not in the coffin.

"That's Brother Banditto!" one of the senior monks exclaimed.

I turned and looked at the exposed face lying in the coffin. The monk was absolutely right.

It was just as I had suspected.

"Then where the hell is Nong Noi?" the abbot demanded, on the way to losing his mind entirely. As if I was supposed to know the answer.

"We'll find him," I said with more confidence than I felt.

"You'll find him?" he repeated, incredulous, his voice rising. "You'll find him? You bloody well will find him, you moron! And you bloody better do it fast before we become the laughing stock of Bangkok!"

"You might consider calming down," I said quietly. "You are, after all, the abbot, and you're making an ass of yourself."

This had the desired effect. He looked around, his bug eyes wide and disbelieving, wondering who had overhear, who had seen him with his robes, as it were, down around his ankles.

"Ananda, this is madness!" he exclaimed quietly. "We've got to do something!"

"And we will," I said. "First, I want to examine this body. Secondly, we're going to call the police and hope they try a little harder this time to figure out what happened. Thirdly, I'm going to go through your personal files on all the monks. And in between all of that, we're going to find a missing dead body of a seventeen-year-old boy and cremate it before anyone figures out what's going on, or his spirit comes back and decides to start haunting this monastery."

"My files?" he asked, frowning, ignoring everything else I had said.

"Yes," I said. "Your personal files. The ones you keep on all of us."

"But why?"

"Because one of us is a murderer, and if we don't figure out who it is, we might wind up with even more dead bodies than we have now."

"A murderer?"

The abbot was sometimes so dense I was left wondering how he got to be an abbot in the first place. "Yes," I said, too forcefully. "A murderer. You don't think it's one of the temple boys, do you? Or the woman out front selling bananas, Mrs.

Nuan? You don't think people are coming up dead because it's fashionable? There's a killer out there, and it's a monk. It's one of us. And we have to figure out who it is before he strikes again."

I turned him around so that he could see the almost 300 souls milling around at the base of the crematorium. "Now, you're going to tell those folks to go on about their business, that we have a small problem, and that Nong Noi will be cremated tomorrow. You're not going to answer any questions because you don't have to — you're the abbot, remember? You're going to speak quietly and hope that the folks from Thai Rath don't hear you. And you're going to do it now before they start coming up here wanting to know what's going on."

I gave him a little push. He descended the stairs slowly, a bit dazed, gathering the monks around and telling them to go on about their business.

All the monks left except Brother Suchinno and his two young assistants.

"I'm going to need your help," I said quietly, looking to Suchinno and his helpers, "and I'm going to need you to keep your mouths shut about what we're going to do. Do I have your word on that?"

The looks I received said I did.

"I need to examine this body, so we're going to carry the coffin back to the death room."

Brother Suchinno instructed his young charges to get on either end of the coffin and the three of them carried it back down the stairs and off to the death room. I followed behind.

There was an odor of death in the air, but then there always was around the crematorium. Some monks, wanting to meditate on death, actually climb inside the crematorium where the bodies are burned so that they can visualize their own death, as a way to prepare for it. I did it myself once and decided I didn't much like it.

The odor was not unfamiliar, but today it seemed rather too strong. Burned bodies have a certain death smell, similar to that of a dead body, but not exactly. What I smelled seemed to be a combination of both.

I stopped on the stairs and turned around, looking back up to the crematorium. There were four slots where coffins could be put inside for burning. The crematorium itself had two chambers with two slots each, and two bodies could be cremated at once, if so desired, though this was rarely done. The two chambers run side by side, with the slots stacked one on top of the other.

I walked back up the steps and looked around. I saw two beetles at the base of the crematorium, and alarm bells went off. Further up, the door that was to receive the coffin and body of Nong Noi had been closed. I opened it, looked inside. It had two tracks, long iron rails, on which the coffin could be placed and rolled inside. There was a long iron tray beneath these tracks to collect the ashes, which most families wanted to keep.

The cremation process took about three hours in all with modern crematoriums, like our own, which ran on natural gas, and got extremely hot. Before the oven was fired, an alarm was sounded — on funeral days, one heard that alarm about five minutes before the cremation was to begin. It was a warning: To mourners, that they should gather around because the cremation was about to begin, and to anyone inside the crematorium — like a meditating monk, for example — that they should get out lest they wanted to burn to death. Once those doors were closed and the oven fired, the game was over.

If you wanted to kill someone, or dispose of a body, the crematorium was the perfect place to do it.

I closed the bottom slot and looked at the top one, just above it, and suddenly I knew where Nong Noi's body had been put.

I turned away from the doors, feeling sick to my stomach. I was about ten meters up in the air on the crematorium platform, and I could see the monastery complex spread out around me. I could see trees in the back, the angular temple roof with its red tiles, the imposing, rather ugly structure of the main dormitory.

I turned back, looking at the door. I didn't want to open it, if truth be told. Was I getting soft in my old age? Perhaps. Quiet days of meditation and tranquility were not exactly conducive to preparing one for life's harsher realities.

With sudden resolve, I reached up and grabbed hold of the handle to the top slot and turned it, pulling the door open and stepping back quickly. Nong Noi's legs flopped out of the door and hung downwards at an unnatural angle and someone, somewhere, screamed.

Five

When a person dies, an undertaker is usually called, but not always right away. Most people die at home, especially the elderly. Their bodies are arranged properly on a bed, and a sheet or blanket are pulled up to their chin. For the next few hours, or perhaps through the night, relatives pay their respects.

But eventually the undertaker had to be called. This man went to the home in a small, covered truck, carrying all the tools and equipment he would need to help relatives wash and dress the body, and prepare it for the time it would spend in the coffin. He brings along the coffin, for that matter, and flower arrangements, and whatever else the family requires.

If the deceased dies at a hospital, the same procedure takes place, only the undertaker goes to the hospital in question to help the relatives retrieve the body from the morgue, prepare it, and then ferry it to a temple, where it remains for a certain number of days while funeral rites and rituals are carried out.

Monks are always called, during this time, to assist the relatives, and to sit with the coffin as it is ferried to the temple. On a sad occasion such as death, an even number of monks are in attendance, in accordance with an old superstition. Happy occasions require an odd number of monks; sad occasions require an even number of monks.

When a monk dies, or when we were called upon to prepare bodies for burial as we sometimes are, the bodies are taken to the death room, not far from the crematorium, which is filled with coffins and all the other paraphernalia of death — plastic flower arrangements, the bolts of string used during the funeral rituals, the saw-horses upon which the coffins are placed, and so on.

There was no getting around the fact that the death room smelled, and I did my best to be detached and not notice it, but as I stood with the abbot and Brother Suchinno and his assistants, surveying the two bodies before us, I had the feeling I might actually be sick.

"Maybe we could open the door," I suggested. Brother Suchinno instructed Brother Chittasangwaro to open the door and stand by it, lest anyone should wander inside.

The flow of fresh air helped somewhat.

My first instinct had been to call Lt. Somchai and let him know there had been a development in the case that he should probably investigate for himself. But the abbot had put forward a different idea. He had called Chao. So now we were all waiting for Chao to arrive with his entourage. I had not been very happy with this idea, and had made no effort to disguise it. I was increasingly getting the feeling that Major General Chao and his undercover operation were nothing but trouble, and I was angry that the abbot had allowed any such thing to be conducted at our monastery without at least informing some of us as to what was going on. The whole thing smacked of double-dealing and falsity.

I wanted to examine Banditto's body myself. Thus, Brother Suchinno unwound the sheet covering his body and the first thing that struck me was that he was wearing a sarong, the type we all wore in the evenings when we prepared for bed. These sarongs were wrapped around the waist, two ends tied in a knot at the hip. If he was wearing a sarong, it suggested quite strongly that he died at night or in the late evening just before bedtime. It was just as I had suspected, that the two robes in his cell meant he hadn't gone anywhere at all.

Brother Banditto was — used to be — a strongly built man, light-skinned, somewhere in his mid to late twenties. He had large arms and legs and a solid waist.

I examined the body, working in silence for many minutes, but for the life of me, I couldn't find any cause of death. There were no wounds, no stab marks, no head caved in from being bashed from behind by a solid object, no cuts, no bruises, nothing at all. It was as if the man simply died in his sleep.

Obviously he had not. Someone had put his body in Nong Noi's coffin. Someone had been hoping his death could be disguised, that his body would burn up during Nong Noi's cremation and that we might not notice the extra ashes on the tray that we would collect afterward. And even if we did, what of it? There would be no way to prove where the extra ashes came from, no way to prove they came from Banditto's body.

It introduced a level of complexity to the case that I had not been prepared for. It also suggested we had a very clever killer on our hands and I was absolutely clueless as to who he might be. That he was a monk seemed doubtful. But that he was one of Chao's men seemed almost certain.

Frustrated, I rolled the body over once more, afraid I'd missed something. I poked along the hairline and checked the back of the scalp. I moved down the neck to the broad shoulders. There was a small bruise on the right shoulder, but faint, a bruise which could have resulted from any number of things — bumping into a wall, for example. I moved down the spine, feeling each of the vertebrae. I removed the sarong altogether, moving down the legs, peering at the feet, even the bottoms of the feet, but I could find nothing.

"How did he die?" the abbot asked.

I looked up to him and shook my head. I didn't know.

"What do you mean, you don't know?"

I shrugged helplessly. I wanted to defend myself. I wanted to say I didn't have the proper tools or resources, that I was not a coroner or a forensic scientist, that I'd been out of uniform for eight years, that there was a possibility that I might not be able to figure out what happened at all, either to this man or the boy now lying beside him. But all of that was pride and the business of ego, so I simply said, "I don't know."

From inside the death room, we heard a car pull up — several, in fact — and the young monk manning the door warned us that the police were coming.

I stood, somewhat relieved. Maybe Chao and his men might have better luck.

We heard booted footsteps from outside, and then Chao came into the death room, walking over to where we stood, not offering the customary greeting. Thrown by this breach of etiquette, we remained standing in silence while he peered at the bodies.

Several of his men came in after him. They were smart looking, dressed sharply, shoes shined, revolvers on their hips and a hint of arrogance on their faces.

"Reverend Father," Chao said quietly, now breaking the silence. He looked at the abbot, and it seemed to me there were secrets passing between them. "How is it that you managed to wind up with two dead bodies on your hands?"

The abbot grinned with embarrassment, and I could see the look of a fawning sycophant before a donor steal over his features. Wealth and power had arrived, and the abbot knew his place.

"Maybe Father Ananda should explain," he said, looking to me, shrugging helplessly. "Father Ananda was once a police officer," he added, as if that explained everything, as if that transferred his responsibility onto my shoulders.

Chao turned to look at me, measuring me with his eyes. I decided I did not like this man, and I was surprised that the abbot called him, and suspicious as to the reasons why. The abbot said Chao had been very generous indeed — to the tune of more than a million baht. But where does man on the salary of police major general get that kind of money? Not, I suspected, from laying down the law.

"Perhaps you could brief me," the man said, not taking away his eyes.

I did. I gave him an abridged version of what had happened at the monastery since the morning when we had discovered Nong Noi's body.

I did not tell him about the evidence I had collected, nor where I had put it. The last thing I needed was some pompous police major general taking away my evidence and perhaps conveniently losing it. I also did not tell him about my interviews, or what I had learned concerning suspicions in the community that some of our monks were selling drugs. That sort of information had to be verified before one began discussing it with outsiders. And if Chao was somehow involved, I didn't want to tip my hand. I didn't want him to know that I had caught on to the game.

During the whole time, Chao never took his eyes away from mine. When I was finished he looked long and hard at the abbot, who withered under his gaze and seemed like he would prefer to collapse in on himself and disappear.

Chao then ordered one of his men, Lt. Aye, to examine the bodies, and watched over his shoulder while the young officer went to work.

They began with Nong Noi.

"Cigarette burns, obviously," Lt. Aye said quietly, pointing to Nong Noi's chest.

Chao nodded.

"Something was in his mouth," Aye added, putting fingers on Nong Noi's jaw and moving it slightly, pulling the lip back to expose the teeth. He scraped at the teeth with a fingernail, showed something to Chao. "Candle wax?"

Again, Chao nodded.

For long minutes, they went over Nong Noi's body, missing absolutely nothing, and finding previous wounds that I had not, and I could see that Chao was mentoring his young officer, teaching-by-doing, looking over his shoulder but staying out of the way.

They examined Brother Banditto in just as thorough a manner, and came away just as stumped as I had been, and yet Chao instructed Aye to roll the man over on his belly, and he bent close for long moments, peering at the small bruise on the man's shoulder.

He then called for a light and a magnifying glass contraption that looked like a small box. He placed this box over the wound, shining the light through it, and I could see something curious swim into view: A small hole, like a pinprick.

"What do you think?" Chao asked his officer.

"It looks like a needle mark, an injection site."

Chao nodded and then stood up. He'd seen enough of the bodies.

"I'm wondering how the bodies were switched," I said.

"I am, too," Chao said. "Who prepared Nong Noi's body?"

Brother Suchinno had, and he said so, looking now a bit ashen-faced and uncertain of himself.

"That morning, when the body was discovered, after the police were through with their investigation, we brought it here," he said. "My assistants and I washed it properly and wrapped it in a sheet, and then we waited for the abbot to come. The abbot said some prayers, blessed the body, and we left it here for the remainder of the day, so that anyone who wanted to pay their respects could come and do so. We weren't sure that anyone would, but we wanted to let the body lie in state anyway. We lit the large candle and the incense sticks, like we always do, and we left it like that."

"Did anyone come?" I asked.

"It seems several of the monks did, yes, mostly the older ones, coming to say prayers or just sit with the body. I thought they felt sorry for the boy. I did myself, for that matter, and I lit some incense sticks for him."

"So anyone could have come into this room on that day?" I asked.

Suchinno nodded.

"And then what?"

"That evening," Suchinno said, "we put the body in the coffin and took it to the funeral hall, for the usual chants and such. I think we did that about three in the afternoon or so, because the chants begin at four."

"Can you show us the coffin?" Chao asked.

Suchinno did, and we gathered around it.

"I've already looked," Suchinno said. "There don't seem to be any signs that it was tampered with, that someone pried up the lid and put another body in it. I mean, I just don't understand it. I don't see how it could be done."

I looked around. There was a stack of coffins lined against the left wall, two and sometimes three deep.

"Do we know if all these are accounted for?" I asked.

Suchinno didn't understand.

"How many of these do we have? Do we keep a record?"

"Yes, we do," Suchinno said. "Salisangwaro, go fetch the records, will you?"

His assistant hurried off.

"You're wondering if one was added?" Chao asked, coming to stand beside me.

"No," I said. "I'm wondering if there wasn't already a body in one of these coffins when Nong Noi was brought it here. Sometime during the day, the killer could have come in here and switched the bodies. It would have been risky, but it wouldn't have taken too long. He might have done it just at 11 a.m., when the monks eat lunch, and it wasn't likely anyone would be coming here. If both bodies had been wrapped in sheets, who would know the difference? And then, at some point, probably at night, the killer could have put the boy's body in the crematorium, in the upper slot, knowing the bottom slot would be used. Both bodies would have been burned, and no one would ever know."

"I see what you're getting at," Chao said. "But then someone had to have a key to get into this room."

Salisangwaro returned, and he and Suchinno quickly counted up the coffins and compared it to their records.

"They're all accounted for," Suchinno said. "We have just as many as we should have."

Lt. Aye stood beside me. "It strikes me as a bit complicated," he said. "Why bother switching the bodies and risk being caught? I mean, there had to be some reason for it."

He had a point.

I looked at the two bodies lying on the floor. One was clearly bigger than the other — heavier, stockier, a man, not a boy, and thus not as easy to move about.

"Maybe," I said, "the killer didn't think he could get Banditto's body into the crematorium slot. He would have to lift it up and push it in there. As it was, he didn't do a very good job of getting Nong Noi's body in there."

"And what does that suggest?" Chao asked, and I could tell by the smile on his face that he already knew.

His men gathered around.

"We're looking for a short killer?" one of them said, not intending to be funny.

We chuckled.

"Or a weak one," Lt. Aye said, "someone who doesn't have the physical strength to lift a man's body that high."

"Like one of the boys," Suchinno said.

He had a point.

"They often send those boys to help me," Suchinno said quietly. "They're not much good when it comes to real work. They can do laundry and stuff, but if have to haul things around or something that requires putting your back into, they're not much good."

Chao nodded.

"We're looking for a killer who isn't that strong, in other words," I said.

Again he nodded.

I didn't want the killer to be one of our boys.

"But the crime itself," Lt. Aye pointed out, "doesn't seem to be the work of a young boy, if you don't mind my saying. It's too sophisticated."

That was also true.

"So maybe we're looking for a monk who isn't very strong," he said, giving me a sideways glance.

I thought of Brother Kittisaro, the office secretary, for some reason, with his delicate features and wire rim glasses.

Six

Chao asked, "Can you show me the monastery grounds?"
I was glad for a chance to leave the death room and its smell.

"I'd like to see the bathroom where you found the boy," he said.

I began walking.

"Why did you leave?" he asked as we strolled down the footpath through the midst of the kutis.

"Leave?" I asked.

"The police department," he added.

"I needed a change," I said.

"Have you found what you were looking for?"

"Perhaps."

We stopped when we arrived at the bathroom where Nong Noi had been found, and for a long time Chao did nothing but look at the outside of the bathroom as well as the surrounding area, and then back up the footpath we had traveled to get there.

"You found no footprints?" he asked.

I nodded.

"Then someone carried the body here, or the boy was murdered here?"

"I don't know."

"Unless it was done in one of these kutis nearby, I would have trouble believing the killer actually carried a dead body all this way."

I could only agree.

"So what are the two things we're looking for, brother monk?" he asked, giving me a friendly look.

"Motive and opportunity," I responded. Did he think I was a rookie in need of mentoring?

"Who had the opportunity to kill the boy?" he asked, then answered his own question. "Someone in one of these kutis is the most likely answer. He would have had privacy, could have carried the body over here without much risk of being seen. So that leaves the motive."

He looked at me, as if suggesting that I should fill in the blanks, provide my thinking, but I was not willing to be drawn.

"Surely you have some idea?" he said.

I shrugged.

"You don't trust me." It was a statement.

I shrugged again.

"If I didn't know better, I would think you were hiding things from me. If I'm going to be any help here, I'm going to need your co-operation."

He was not pleading, merely stating the facts.

"So it's going to be business as usual?" he asked quietly, giving me his eyes. "Standard operating procedure. Who are you covering up for, monk? Are you going to make some money off this situation? Is that it? Or maybe you're the one who did it?"

I had to laugh at his cheek. "Maybe I was just waiting to see how much you could be trusted. And anyway, you're the investigating officer. What does it matter what I think?'

"I should very much like to know what you think," he said.

"I don't know what to think, to be honest. We started off with one dead body, now we've got two. There doesn't seem to be any connection between the victims. We don't have any smoking guns pointing straight at the perpetrator. So, I don't know what to tell you. And anyway, my investigation has only just begun, and given the number of potential suspects, it could be a long time before I get anywhere. Maybe there just isn't much to tell you."

He seemed to be satisfied by this response. A thoughtful look stole across his face.

"Let me tell you what I see," he said. "From the examination of the bodies it seems that the boy might have been tortured before he died — the cigarette burns. Torture suggests that he knew something, or he was involved in something. What did he know? What was he involved in? I assume that you're looking into the boy's past, his history, who he was, what it was that might have got him killed, the sort of people he associated with, that sort of thing.

"Secondly, the monk, unlike the boy, was not tortured. There are no obvious signs of injury on his body, except that small bruise, which I'm willing to gamble is an injection site. It's on his back — it looks like someone came up behind him and stabbed him. Perhaps had a syringe full of heroin — I hear it's not hard to come by in this part of town. Could have been rat poison, for that matter. Could have been air — that will kill you just as easily. But that suggests a bit of cowardice, doesn't it, the coming from behind? It's not at all like what was done to the boy, the gouging out of his eyes, the torture, the stuffing of a candle in his mouth.

"So, what we have here are two dead bodies, two very different means of death. That suggests there might be two killers. The first killing was an act of passion, of anger, of rage, of hate. The body seems almost deliberately defiled. Even dumping it in a bathroom is symbolic — what else do you dump in a bathroom?"

I made a face.

"But the second murder is much different, isn't it? It's not about power, it's not about rage, it's about stealth, about coming up from behind someone and stabbing him with a syringe, a cowardly crime, almost a womanly crime, as if the killer was afraid that he wouldn't be able to overpower the victim.

"And the manner of disposing of the monk's body — switching it with the boy — why, that's very clever indeed. This killer didn't want the body found, didn't want to be caught. Didn't want anyone to know what he had done. Do you see what I'm getting at here?"

I did. Did we have two killers on our hands?

"Perhaps Brother Banditto came across the killer, saw what he had done — and got himself killed for it?" I suggested.

"That's a very real possibility. And even that's suggestive. It says that someone was very angry with the boy — his killing seems almost like it was personal. But the boy was small, perhaps defenseless. The murdered monk, on the other hand, was not small and defenseless, so maybe our killer was afraid of him, and came up behind him and stabbed him."

He approached the bathroom, poked his head through the door, coming away with an expressionless face. "Do you believe in justice, brother monk?"

I wasn't sure I had heard the question correctly. Most police officers don't stand around discussing philosophy at a crime scene. "I believe in karma," I said, and that was true. "I believe bad actions will have bad results, and one day you will answer for them, either in this life or in some other life."

"But that's not really what I meant. Do you believe in the Thai system of justice?"

I couldn't help but laugh. I knew the police tried, but they were often arrayed against forces they could not control. Wealth, power, influence — the police were often at their mercy.

To many people, it seemed laws were enacted simply to give police increased opportunities to exhort money from those whom they caught breaking them. No law, no matter how serious, could not be broken with impunity if one greased the right palms with the right amount of money. Witnesses could be bought off or intimidated, evidence lost, convictions overturned, honest judges executed — it was really quite amazing what money was capable of purchasing in our part of the world.

Each month, the average police officer found an envelope stuffed with cash in his desk. If he accepted it, took the money out of the envelope and put it in his pocket, spent it, he became a silent partner in the whole enterprise. Given his small salary, what real choice was there?

I had participated myself, allowing myself to rationalize my behavior in all sorts of ways until I reached a point where I could no longer do so.

He nodded, understanding the reason why I was so openly scoffing at his question. "I respond to crime scenes so that I can teach my men how to properly investigate a death or a violent crime. I was educated abroad, and the things they're doing today in forensic science are really quite astonishing. We're so far behind I don't see how we will ever catch up. But we have to try, don't we? I'm well aware that the police are viewed as corrupt and unprofessional, and in many cases, they are. But, again, we have to do what we can with what we have. It's a process of education, mostly, isn't it? But the old ways die hard. That's why I asked you why you left the department. Were you disillusioned? Sick of the corruption? Unwilling to participate? If so, I can certainly understand. And the ironic thing is that we need men like you, men with conscience, men who want things to change, who are tired of the old ways, tired of the corruption. I suppose what I'm trying to figure out is what side of the law you're on. The status quo? Or the side of justice? If you really want to figure out what happened here, who killed these people, then you're going to have to be honest with me."

A part of me was thrilled to hear such words from a police official. That part of me believed very much in justice, hoped for change, for a professional police force, a professional, honest government, an end to corruption and deceit and hypocrisy, an end to routine injustices inflicted on poor people by civil servants of every stripe and color. The old ways were already changing, but corruption was so deeply entrenched in some places that it did not seem possible there would ever come a time when we would be free of it. It wasn't even the corruption itself that bothered me. It was the fact that the poor, the little people, the ones least able to afford to grease the wheels, these were the ones "justice" was administered to. It was people such as these that filled our prisons. What they could not pay for in cash, they paid with their bodies and their souls. And when they needed the protection of the police, that protection was often not forthcoming. Those most at risk were the most exploited and least helped. The Lord Buddha himself had spoken long and eloquently on many of these matters, and his words had opened my eyes in very many ways.

But then we were interrupted by a call that came over Chao's radio. He turned away from me to answer it.

"They've found something," he said, putting his radio away and giving me a curious glance.

Wordless, I followed.

Seven

We stood in front of the kuti that belonged to Brother Satchapalo.

Chao stood by the side of the kuti looking down at the ground where a syringe had been discovered. His officers had carefully screened off the area and were now searching the kuti itself.

The syringe could very well be the one used to kill Brother Banditto. If Brother Satchapalo was the killer, he might have tossed the syringe aside and forgotten about it after the killing, too preoccupied with hiding the body.

Monks were now congregating around the kuti, wanting to know what was happening.

The search of Brother Satchapalo's kuti, though, turned up nothing, and there was really no reason to believe he had anything to do with the murders. It might have been his dumb luck to have the kuti next to which the killer tossed the syringe. He denied knowing anything about the syringe and seemed just as bewildered as the rest of us.

It was nearly 9 p.m. by the time Chao and his men left. They had conducted quick interviews of all the monks, even the abbot. They had photographed the bodies. They had searched all the main buildings.

No one had been arrested, and Chao offered no clue as to his thinking concerning who might have been responsible for the crimes.

The abbot ordered the younger monks to go to bed immediately, and to remain in their cells until the morning bell. The senior monks were ordered to congregate in the prayer hall. Brother Khantiphalo was told to choose an assistant from among the senior monks to help him watch over the boys, who were likewise to go to their dorm immediately and remain there until breakfast tomorrow. The gates out front were to be locked and there was no to be no coming and going.

I took up stride next to Brother Thammarato as we headed for the main prayer hall.

"Hasn't been a lock-down like this since ever I could remember," the older man said sadly.

"It may be a little too late," I replied.

In the main prayer hall we sat down, in no particular order, arranging ourselves around the abbot, who clearly had things on his mind that he wanted to share.

Senior monks are those who have been in the robes for more than five years. They're usually about a few dozen in any given monastic population. Lots of men take the robes for a week or two, or three months, or even a year, but not many stay in them. Consequently, we have a lot of junior monks, and whenever there is trouble to speak of, it usually has something to do with them.

I looked at my fellow monks, my religious brothers. There was Brother Suchinno, Brother Thammarato, Brother Kittisaro , the learned Brother Chittakhutto, about thirty in all, whom I had known and lived with for years. I did not think any of them capable of murder.

"Monks," the abbot said, standing up and addressing us. "We're in trouble."

He gave us his eyes, looking around and seeming rather helpless and forlorn. He was the abbot, of course, but abbots aeren't invincible and don't always have all the answers. Our abbot was human enough not to pretend otherwise.

"If there's anything you can think of, please share it with us. If you know what happened to Brother Banditto, to the boy, if you suspect something, if you've seen anything odd going on — anything at all — now's the time to speak up.

"I've called you all here because I've known all of you for many, many years, and I don't believe anyone sitting in this room is capable of murder. But we have a lot of junior monks out there, brothers, whom we don't always know so well. And it seems to me one of those junior monks must be the murderer we're looking for. So if you've seen anything — anything at all — that strikes you as odd or unusual, I want to stand up and say so."

He let his eyes wander over us.

"But first, I'd like Ananda to tell us about his investigation," he added. "Perhaps something he says will ring a bell with one of you. Maybe he can give you a better idea of the sorts of things we're looking for."

The abbot quieted, and the eyes in the room turned toward me.

I was being put on the spot but there was certainly good cause. "Maybe I'd better start at the beginning," I said, and I did: I started with the discovery of Nong Noi's body, and told the brothers everything I knew and everything I had done. I told them about the reporter for Thai Rath, and the suspicions that there was drug selling going on at the temple — there was an angry response to this, but I reassured them that I was just conveying what was being said about us around the neighborhood. I told them about my conversation with Brother Khantiphalo concerning Nong Noi, his history, the fact that he was not well liked. I told them about the medal I had found, the evidence I had collected and hidden away, and my rather strange conversation with Chao that evening. I told them about Noot and the four boys and the discovery of drugs among their things. I told them about my search of

Banditto's kuti, which likewise turned up drugs. I told them about our suspicions that someone had stabbed Banditto with a syringe, whether full of heroin — enough to overdose — or even oxygen, we did not know, but that there seemed to be no other apparent cause of death. I told them about my visit to Noi's aunt, Jut, and what she had said about him. I told them everything I could think of.

When I finished, the monks all began to speak at once — suddenly, it seemed, everyone had seen something or other that might be of interest.

"One at a time," the abbot said, standing up and holding out his hands. "One at a time, please."

I received a number of comments:

"I saw Nong Noi once at night out by the kutis. He was crying."

"I saw Nong Noi getting on a motorcycle and roaring off."

"I saw Nong Noi coming out of the brother's cloister in the main dormitory — I was wondering what he had been doing in there."

"I saw one of those boys with a mobile phone."

"I saw Banditto arguing with Satchapalo one day, not too long ago. Now that syringe turns up next to Satchapalo's kuti ..."

"I saw one of the boys hanging around Chutintharo's kuti."

"I saw one of those boys in Banditto's kuti — he was naked. I asked him what he thought he was doing. He said he was changing and he put on his clothes and ran off. I thought it very odd."

"I saw that red-headed kid talking to Banditto."

On and on it went.

By the time we were through, I had a list of junior monks that needed to be talked to — and a nagging suspicion that not all of them were doing their best to fulfill the precepts. I had all sorts of reasons to suspect Chao's men — Satchapalo,

Chutintharo, Panyathiro. But what I didn't have was an explanation of the facts that made sense, that put the pieces together — and that would point me in the direction of the killer.

EIGHT

I was exhausted as I made my way back to my kuti. The encounter with Chao left me confused. The man was obviously not a blithering idiot. I wanted to believe he was honest, sincere, good hearted. I wanted to believe that men like him would transform the police, and make my former profession one of honor and respect.

And yet, I was sceptical. Smooth talkers we had in abundance. As the abbot liked to say, the proof was in the pudding. It isn't what a man says, but what he does.

If Chao were corrupt, why wouldn't he do everything by the book, giving no reason for anyone to suspect him of anything? The end result would strengthen his hand. And anyway, the end result would be the same: His interests would be protected, the killer — or killers — would go free, and no one would ever be the wiser. He could, in fact, do nothing now but sit on the case, charging no one, getting to the bottom of nothing, and that would be just fine as far as his interests were concerned. If he was running some sort of drug operation out of our temple, that would make perfect sense.

And, for that matter, *was* he running some sort of drug operation out of our temple? Was he just another corrupt higher-up running a drug gang on the side? Were Satchapalo and the others members of his gang on the run from the law, and hiding out in our temple under the cover of orange robes and pseudo respectability?

I hoped not. To take the robes with such devious intentions would automatically make one's ordination to the monkhood invalid. Such a man would not be a monk, no matter what rituals he went through, or whether he wore the robes or not. The monkhood had to do with purity of intention and a genuine interest to learn and strive to live the Lord Buddha's teachings. If one took to the robes for other reasons, his actions were pointless and fruitless.

The night air was cool, and the rainy season would not be long in coming now. I loved the rains, actually. Of course they were a nuisance, and streets and small alleys would be flooded and traffic would grind to a halt, but they were also cleansing, in a way, and the storms themselves were magnificent — huge, rumbling clouds of thunder and lightning, downpours that appeared suddenly and lasted for hours, leaving streets littered with refuse. It was the only time of year that the season actually changed, that something different happened. Normally it was heat and humidity and the sun beating down and the only difference was between hot and hotter. At least with the rains, the temperature plunged and it sometimes actually got chilly.

When I arrived at my kuti, I was surprised — and a little unnerved — to see Brother Satchapalo sitting on the steps.

"Ananda," he said, standing as I approached.

He was bigger than I, younger, stronger. If he meant to do me bodily harm, he would no doubt succeed.

"What can I do for you?" I asked, trying to maintain a discreet distance between us.

"It's about what I told you before, about the boy," he said quietly. There was no menace about him now, no anger, no tension in his body. "You know who I am now, so I wanted to tell you the rest of it."

"And who are you, exactly?" I asked.

"I'm a police officer."

I waited for him to continue.

"That boy came to my kuti many times, Ananda. He was one of the ones making deliveries. I was trying to befriend him, trying to figure out what he was up to. I wanted to tell you that in case you got any ideas, or someone else told you that he had been to my kuti more than once — trying to save you from having to chase your tail around, I guess. But as far as what happened to him, I haven't got a clue. I just assumed one of the brothers got irritated with him — that was really easy to do — and whacked him. The thing is, I had no reason to kill him. Just the opposite. I needed him to lead me to the bigger fish. I didn't much care for him personally – his behavior was childish and stupid – but I needed him."

I listened to this in silence.

"You don't trust me, do you?" he asked.

I didn't, but there was no point in saying so. "I'm wondering if you know what happened to Brother Banditto?" I asked.

He gave me a genuinely puzzled look and said he didn't know.

"You were one of those closest to him," I pointed out. "Did he have any enemies? Were the four of you involved in something that got him killed?"

He shrugged. For a police officer who had lost a comrade, he seemed remarkably cool.

"If you think of something, let me know," I said.

He nodded and walked away.

CHAPTER FIVE

"The craving of the man addicted to careless living grows like a Maluva creeper. He jumps hither and thither, like a monkey in the forest looking for fruit."

The Lord Buddha. From the Dhammapada, #334.

One

After breakfast the following morning, I collected Jak, and we went to the front gates and turned left, heading to the small alley where I had seen Satchapalo and the others go the day before. I wanted to check out the house they were visiting. If they were police officers, the house was obviously some sort of headquarters, and I would be allowed entrance.

"We're going to that house?" Jak asked, hesitant.

I nodded.

"Is it safe, Father Ananda?"

"Of course it is," I said, though I was none too sure.

We walked down the main road and turned into the soi. On a whim — and since I was dressed in robes — I decided to ask some of the vendors what they thought of our "monks."

The first, a man who sold dried fish, snorted. "No offense, Reverend Father, but they're not the most friendly monks I've seen. Of course, this is Bangkok and all, and you don't expect people to be very friendly. But these monks strike me as odd."

"How?" I asked, intrigued.

"Well," he said, laughing, "I asked once for a blessing from one of them — the tall one — and he rattled off the Taking of the Precepts Chant, as if I wouldn't know the difference. I'm not an educated man, but I've received enough blessings to know one when I hear one. After that, I was quite suspicious, to tell you the truth."

If these men weren't monks and really were police officers, I would expect them to make mistakes like that. But what I needed to figure out was whether or not they were police officers at all. I had a feeling we were being rolled. There had to be some way I could get to the bottom of the question. If we were being rolled, it could turn out that Nong Noi knew about it and threatened to expose them — and that would have given them a powerful motive to kill him.

I talked to more vendors, working my way slowly down the street. Most seemed hesitant, as if they expected all the monks from Wat Mahanat to be as unfriendly as their daily visitors were. I head many more tales about curious slip-ups.

We went down to the end of the street and Jak was now hanging back, afraid to go further.

"Tell you what," I said. "Why don't you wait for me here? If I don't return, if you think there's some trouble, you go get the abbot and tell him what happened, okay?"

"What if they see you?" he asked.

"What of it?" I replied. "I'm just going to go have a look."

I left him there with a look of consternation on his face.

I was hesitant myself, to be honest. I was no longer a policeman. I had no weapon. If these men were crooked, I could be getting myself into serious trouble.

I walked down the street and looked at the houses on the left side, and the shop houses on the right. In the very first one I saw a man standing in the second-floor window, looking down on me — Brother Satchapalo. When he saw me looking up, he quickly stepped away from the window.

I went up to the door, rang the bell. I didn't know what I was going to say when he, or one of the others, answered, but I wanted to know what they were doing. If they were police officers, what did they have to hide or worry about?

I waited for a long minute, before ringing the bell again. Were they not going to answer?

The front door, and the windows were curtained, and there was no way to see inside.

No one came to the door.

I went back out in front and looked up, but saw no one in the windows.

I returned to the door and rang the bell again, and waited once more. Minutes went by. There was no response. I tried the door on the off chance it might be unlocked, but it was not. I tried the windows too, with no luck.

Brother Satchapalo was not going to answer the door.

I walked away from the shop house, both angry and excited — angry that Satchapalo was playing games with me, and yet excited because his actions demonstrated that he had something to hide.

But what, precisely?

Two

I went to see the abbot. Although it was Sunday, he was in his office, tending to paperwork.

"How do we know these men are really police officers?" I asked.

"Don't start with me," the abbot said, annoyed.

"I think we need to be certain, Reverend Father."

"If they are police officers, then you're just making a fool of yourself," he said.

"But if they're not, then they're making a fool of you and all the rest of us. Have you considered that?"

He looked uncomfortable.

"I want to see their files. Surely you must have some record of who they are?"

He looked even more uncomfortable.

"Reverend Father, you need to ask yourself about these men. If they're not police officers, then what are they, and what are they doing at your monastery? Do you know what a scandal that could be, if it was discovered monks were running a drug operation out of this monastery and temple? Have you considered what that would do to your program funding?"

"I was told not to meddle," the abbot said.

"By whom?"

"Chao."

"Since when do you answer to Chao?" I asked. "Is it possible that you don't want to open this particular can because you might find out that it is indeed full of worms?"

He shook his head, avoided my eyes. "Ananda, if these people aren't police officers, then what does that say about me? What does that say about my management of this temple? I'll be called out onto the carpet."

So that was the problem.

"But if you beat them at their game, and expose them," I said, "then you'll look like a hero, won't you? And if this is going on at other temples, you could be exposing a lot of fraudulent monks. If anything, people would be grateful, wouldn't they?"

He did not seem to buy this line of argument, but knew he had to do something. He opened the bottom drawer to his desk and pulled out a set of files.

"These are the files," he said quietly. "Chao told me not to put them with the others, to keep them separate, and not let anyone see them, lest his men be exposed, their cover blown, something to that effect." He slid the files across the desk. "I'm trusting you, Ananda, not to make things worse than they already are, or might be. Do you understand?"

"Perfectly," I said, looking through the files, noting right away that all the men came from the North. "I'm going to need these for a while."

"You're going to take them with you?"

"Just a day or two."

Three

"Where are we going now?"

Jak had just returned from fetching more money — the treasurer was probably thinking I had gone mad — and seemed out of sorts.

"To the police station," I said. "Why are you so down in the mouth?"

He gave me a large frowned and looked away.

We boarded another bus.

"What is it?" I pressed.

"They call me One-Leg Jak," he said miserably. "They're always calling me that. I hate it."

"Who are they?" I asked.

"The other guys," he answered.

Kids had a cruelty that was disturbing. I didn't know what to say in response to this, so said nothing. It was one of life's sad realities that he was going to have to get used to, whether it was fair or not.

Lt. Somchai was not in, but I asked the receptionist to page him and ask him to come, telling her it was urgent. I received a hesitant look.

"It's urgent," I repeated.

"Can't you just talk to him on the phone?" she suggested.

"He needs to come here. We need to check something, and right away."

Reluctantly, she agreed, and I was ushered into the waiting room, where I sat for about thirty minutes until Lt. Somchai showed up.

"I'm really very sorry to bother you on your day off," I said.

"Never mind," he replied, waving his hand. "I was sitting in the house looking at all my wife's magazines and wondering to do about them. You've given me the perfect reason to think about something else."

I showed him the files I'd been given by the abbot, and asked him whether he could verify whether the men were indeed police officers.

"There's a national database now, isn't there?" I asked.

He nodded. "I need a reason, though, if they're going to give me permission to check."

"These men," I said, nodding at the files, "are supposed to be police officers working undercover at my temple. I don't believe they are. I need to know, one way or the other. If they're not, then I'm willing to bet they were responsible for the death of that boy."

"Working undercover?" he repeated, giving me a puzzled look.

"Exactly," I said. "Supposedly running an anti-narcotics operation, posing as monks."

"But that's illegal."

"Indeed it is."

"Alright, I'll call and see what's what. Give me some time."

He got up and walked away, and I stared around at the other desks — most of them empty now, this being Sunday — and sighed. It seemed like the life I had once had as a police officer was so long ago, and yet it was like yesterday.

Together with Jak, we waited for almost an hour before Somchai returned. The frown on his face told me that my suspicions had been correct.

"These aren't police officers," he said straight away. "They're not even people. They're not registered with the national ID database, in other words. They're fake, all of them — these names and addresses. None of it can be verified."

Pretty much what I had expected.

Four

When I returned to the monastery, Jak was hesitant to part with me. He was smarting from the teasing. My heart went out to him.

"Come along," I said, feeling sorry for him, wanting to give him an excuse to put off, if only for a few hours, the inevitable. His face brightened. We went to the main office.

Kittisaro looked worried, sitting behind his receptionist's desk.

"What is it?" I asked.

He nodded in the direction of the abbot's office. "Chao."

"Chao?"

Kittisaro nodded. "Hopping mad. I thought he was going to jump right out of his skin. They're waiting for you. When he came in, he demanded to know where you were. I told him you went off to the police station — I couldn't lie. He's been in there with the abbot ever since."

Well, I thought, there was no time like the present, and I was dying to know what Chao had to say for himself now.

"Are you sure you want to go in there?" Kittisaro asked, leading me to the door.

"What's the worst that could happen?" I asked.

As soon as the door opened and Chao saw me, he jumped to his feet, coming to stand about three inches from my face. "What right do you have to be interfering with my operation?"

"I beg your pardon," I said.

Kittisaro closed the door quietly and I was left to confront this angry police major general with the abbot staring at me from behind his desk.

"You've been following my men," he said angrily. "Today you went to the house where they have their headquarters. What are you trying to do, expose them? What are the neighbors going to think?"

"I'm not sure I get the point. Why didn't your men just answer the door and tell me to bugger off?"

"That's what I'm telling you now, brother monk! Bugger off! Don't be putting your nose where it doesn't belong. You're jeopardizing a year's worth of work."

Kittisaro was right — Chao was about to jump out of his skin.

"Would you mind getting out of my face," I asked, "and calming down? If there's anyone who needs to be questioned in this room, it's you. And if you can't address me respectfully, you can bugger off yourself."

"Ananda!" the abbot exclaimed, mortified.

"I was assured that everything would be discreet," Chao said, turning to the abbot and giving him an accusing glare.

The abbot seemed helpless.

"Would you mind explaining why the men you've posted here under cover are not police officers at all?" I asked.

He whirled around, turning his angry eyes on me. "What is this nonsense?"

"I checked," I said.

"You checked what?"

"I checked to see whether the men you say are police officers really are police officers. They're not listed with the national database. Would you like to explain that?"

He looked like he might start spitting tacks. "My men are not listed in the database," he said angrily. "Any fool would know that. They're undercover officers. No one has access to their files."

"So you supplied bogus names for your men?"

"I don't have to answer to you," he spat out. He turned to the abbot. "You better rein this fellow in, or I'll have to take my operation elsewhere. And my funding too, for that matter."

I laughed, and he turned around to look at me as if I were mad. "You're going to dangle the misery and suffering of homeless kids in front of an abbot, hoping you can cow him into silence?" I asked. "Into just accepting everything you say, as if we have no right to verify any of the information you provide? How pathetic!"

I saw his hand move toward his waist where his revolver was holstered, and wondered if I had gone too far. Yet I was convinced this man was a fraud, was up to no good, and was involving our monastery in it, and I wasn't about to stand for it.

"Are you going to shoot me?" I asked. "Is that what they taught you over in the States, that if someone questions you, you just shoot them? Or maybe you're not as sick of the old ways as you pretend to be."

"I don't have to listen to this," he sputtered, glaring once more at the abbot. "I told you that no one was to see those files. You've broken our agreement. You're going to have to get your funding somewhere else from now on."

"You're still not answering my questions," I said. I was angry at the tone and manner he was using with the abbot, and I knew his show of bluster was meant to frighten and intimidate. It worked on the abbot. It did not work on me.

He turned to face me. "What questions?"

"Who these men are, for a start," I said. "We have a right to know. I'm also wondering if you're aware that it's a crime to wear the robes of a Buddhist monk if you're not a monk. I'd like to know how you got permission to be excused from that prohibition. I'd like to know what we should tell people when they find out that we have monks walking around here who aren't really monks. I'd also like to know whether or not one of these monks of yours had someone to do with the death of one of our homeless boys. That may not be high on your list of priorities, but it is on mine. If you can't provide any verification for your claims, then I'd like to know exactly what you're up to here at this monastery."

"Don't you know who I am?" he asked quietly — and I fell silent. When you come across someone who starts asking you that question, trouble quickly follows. It's the voice of power and wealth and high status saying get out of the way — or be prepared to pay the price.

"I guess you're not as enlightened as I thought," I said.

He pushed past me and stormed out the door.

"What a nice man," I said, turning to look at the abbot.

"Do you know what you've just done?" he asked, terror on his face.

"Yes," I said. "But do you?"

"What is that supposed to mean?"

"It means you've been letting four men walking around this monastery for a year now. One of them is dead. One of our boys is dead. And by the time we see the back of these people, there might be more dead bodies lying around."

"We have to call the police," he said, worried.

"I already did. Lt. Somchai is looking into Chao and his men. If Chao can't produce anything to back up his claims, he's in trouble. At the very least, we can charge these men with wearing the robes under false pretenses."

The abbot shook his head. "What a damned mess. Ananda, I shouldn't need to tell you to be careful. Of all people, you should know precisely what you're getting into here."

"Because I was a police officer?"

"That, too, but I think you know what I mean."

I did.

I was surprised at the hurt that washed through me as I stood there before the abbot. He looked at me in a way that suggested he pitied me.

I hated that.

"Just be careful," he said quietly.

Five

There was relief on Kittisaro's face when I appeared at his desk — he was cowering behind one of his large computer monitors.

"You're still alive?" he asked.

"I've had worse dressing downs," I admitted.

"I have something for you," he said, handing me a stack of printouts of what appeared to be news reports. "There's a gang in Chiang Rai that gouges out the eyes of informants, anyone who crosses their path basically. When you read those stories, you'll see that they're all related to drug activity — shootings, raids, that sort of stuff. One of the reporters even notes that other cases were similar, that victims were found with their eyes removed, and that it seems to be the work of a gang up there."

"But nowhere else?" I asked.

"I checked. No. There's a lot of stories about shootings and drug-related activities, but only the ones in Chiang Rai talk about bodies being found with their eyes taken out."

I scanned the reports, and he was right.

"Now do you mind telling me what's going on?" he asked.

I looked at him.

"I mean, we have a kid who gets his eyes gouged out, and you've got me on the Internet tracking down this drug gang — I'm putting two and two together. Do you think this gang killed him?"

"You're a genius," I said.

"That may be," Kittisaro said, "but you're not answering my question. How did these people get inside our monastery? Did they climb over the walls at night? And why?"

"Someday I'll tell you the whole story," I said, "but right now you need to track down our brothers with missing files and tell them to report here immediately."

He gave me a puzzled look.

"Just do it," I said.

He got on the phone, paging one of his assistants to go find the brothers in question.

We waited for a long time, and I read through the news reports he had given me. The abbot had yet to emerge from his office — he had been badly shaken.

At length, one of the boys, Yai, came to the office, winded and sweating. "I've looked everywhere," he said to Kittisaro. "I can't find them."

"You looked in their kutis, cells, the dining hall, everywhere?"

"I looked everywhere, Father Kittisaro , out in front, over by the bo tree. They're not here."

"Thanks Yai," Kittisaro said, glancing at me.

Had they flown the coop already?

Kittisaro cleared his throat. "You don't think these brothers are part of that gang, do you?"

I looked at Kittisaro , offering a small smile.

"They're not!" he exclaimed.

"What better place to hide than behind the robes?" I asked.

Six

I was exhausted and ready for bed.

Chao's monks were gone. I had searched their cells and kutis, but they had collected their things and fled the scene. I suspected we wouldn't be seeing them anymore.

I was left with the problem of how to link one of them to Nong Noi's murder. I was also left with the problem of Brother Banditto — who had killed him and why? And if his compatriots had left, how was I going to prove anything one way or the other?

I went inside my kuti and flicked on the light, unwinding my upper robe and laying it aside, now completely out of sorts. It had been a number of days since I had meditated properly, had been calm and collected, gathered in, my mind not hopping from subject to subject like a monkey looking for the perfect banana and jumping from tree to tree to find it.

When I got into this state, I began to make mistakes, not thinking clearly, sometimes being rash, sometimes doing foolish things. My temper wasn't helped by it either, and that day, arguing with Chao, I had felt the strange thrill of anger coursing through my veins — righteous anger, but anger just the same. The feeling of it was almost sexual, the way it swept through the body, with the adrenalin pumping, the emotions heightened. It was, I knew, quite possible to be addicted to anger, to the feeling of it, and to create situations where one could be angry just to experience those feelings. I had often done it myself, and I was not alone.

But this stirring up of the emotions and giving way to them was very unmonk-like business, and I was regretting my actions now. I was going to have to see Father Thammarato again for another confession.

"Paw?"

I heard Jak outside, calling me. What on earth did he want? My first impulse was to shout at him, to tell him to bugger off, that I was tired and in no mood to be bothered — my anger was clearly not finished, looking for other targets, anything at all, to feed on. I resisted that impulse. Instead, I look through the screen door of my kuti and saw him standing at the foot of my stairs.

"Are you alright?" he asked, hair dangling in his eyes, a frown turning his handsome face into one full of doubt and concern.

I was going to answer, but felt a sudden pain in my left ankle, as though something had bitten me, like one of the larger breeds of spider that sometimes found their way inside our kutis, and which could be right nuisances.

I looked down, surprised by the pain of it, stomping my foot in irritation.

A cobra slithered out from behind the stack of books setting by my door, fanning its neck and rearing its head and going for my leg again.

"Shit!" I exclaimed, so completely surprised I didn't know what to do.

"Paw?"

I heard Jak's footsteps coming up the stairs of my kuti, the thud of his strong leg, the softer thud of his weak one.

"Get back!" I shouted.

Snakes — cobras especially — were no strangers to the countryside, but they could also be encountered in the city, even one the size of Bangkok. You would think they would be killed before they could so much as make their way across the first outlying suburb, but somehow they found a way.

I felt suddenly faint. Cobras are dangerously poisonous, their venom fast-acting. But before I even had time to move or respond, the snake struck again, catching me in the calf, and I stumbled over backwards, landing on my backside and letting out an involuntary shout.

"Paw?" Jak was standing at the door, trying to push through it.

"Get back!" I shouted, pushing him away from the door so forcefully that he fell over on the porch with a painful cry of surprise.

The cobra slithered across the floor and I lunged for it, knowing it didn't matter now whether the thing bit me again or not — if I was going to die, I was going to die, and being bitten three times by a cobra is usually enough to do the trick. But the creature was going to die with me, if only because it might bite someone else, like my kuti boy.

The last thing I remembered was wondering not how the snake had gotten into my kuti, but who had put it there. But then blackness took me and I had a sudden, fleeting thought that I was dying, and it didn't seem quite as bad as I thought it would be.

Still, it was bloody inconvenient.

CHAPTER SIX

"Do not think lightly of evil, saying: 'It will not come to me.' Even a water-pot is filled by the falling of drops. Likewise the fool, gathering it drop by drop, fills himself with evil."

The Lord Buddha. From the Dhammapada, #121.

One

There are worse things than dying. Bed pans, for example. I was propped up on one, waiting for the nurse to come and remove it, perfectly embarrassed. It was providing an enormous incentive to get better as quickly as I possibly could.

I was weak, feverish, my body aching. It was hard to get my thoughts to focus. Just when I thought I was feeling better, the nurses came along and gave me medicine — anti-venom therapy, if I had heard correctly — that made me drowsy and foggy and unable to concentrate.

After the attack, Jak raced to get help. Brother Suchinno responded, going to my kuti to find me clutching the cobra. He killed it, and then administered the first aid that had saved my life. He carried me to the front of the monastery where a taxi had been summoned and I was taken to the hospital. He had done all the right things, and none of the wrong things. I owed my life to both of them.

A male nurse came and I remained silent while he did his business. He was gracious, efficient, fast.

Two

When I next woke, it was the morning of the next day. I was feeling a bit more clear-headed.

Jak was camped out in my room, ready to render assistance, and he had plenty of opportunities that day — helping me to the bathroom, fetching things for me to read. I could see he was making an effort not to bother me, not to pester me with questions, to just be there if I needed him.

It was time I made a decision about him.

After lunch, he sat down in the chair next to my bed, engrossed in a novel he had borrowed from Khun Charn.

"You're going to return that, aren't you, when you're finished?" I asked.

He looked up to me, nodding.

"Khun Charn used to be my boss."

He offered me an odd look, as if he could not understand how I had ever had a boss.

"I haven't always been a monk," I said.

"You used to be a police officer," he said.

"Khun Charn was my superior. He's a good man, a good man to know, a good friend to have. So don't forget to return his book, okay? He thinks boys who read books are the best thing since traffic expressways."

"I won't forget," he said earnestly.

His hair fell into his eyes, reminding me of my son, who would now be a few years older than Jak — twenty or twenty-one or so, had he lived. What would he have become? A police officer like his dad? A scholar? A scientist? A football player?

"What is it, Father Ananda?" Jak asked, bending forward and looking at me strangely.

For so long, I had been punishing this boy, comparing him — unfairly — to my dead son, sometimes pushing him away, sometimes pulling him close, wanting to love him, to give him the love that all boys deserve, to be the father he didn't have, to fill up the empty spaces in his life in whatever way I could. But I was terrified; afraid I would fail him, as I had failed my own son.

Jak was not my official kuti boy — I had refused to accept one. So he was my kuti boy in all respects, yet lacked the proper title. It was just one more bit of hardness on my part that I had to rectify.

"Maybe it's time you became my kuti boy, right and proper," I said quietly, giving him my eyes.

I was surprised by the fear that flashed across his features, as if he dared not hope he was hearing correctly. It made me feel bad about myself — as it should. I was like a crotchety old man clinging to my past, rather than trying to live in the present and accept the many wonderful things it had to offer, too busy nursing my own wounds to see the wounds of others.

"I'll do my best if you will," I said. "If you can put up with me, that is."

He lowered his head and wouldn't let me see his face. I could tell by the shaking of his shoulders that he was crying.

"It's alright," I said, reduced to helplessness — my son's tears had always done that to me. It didn't matter what the problem was. A scraped knee was just as a bad as taking a beating at the hands of the grade school bully. To see him helpless, so full of hurt, smarting from one of life's blows — it took the wind right out of my sails.

I shifted myself on the bed so I could reach over to Jak and pull him a bit closer, putting my hands clumsily on his shoulders, telling him everything was going to be alright. I wanted to believe that was true, but I wasn't sure.

Three

Later that night, with Jak curled up on the couch fast asleep, I lay awake and ran all the events through my mind, trying to find something I had overlooked, trying to make a picture out of the many pieces I had been given.

There was no denying the fact that Nong Noi and Brother Banditto had been killed, perhaps on the same night. What had happened on that night? Had Banditto killed Nong Noi? Or had Banditto seen Nong Noi's killer, and tried to intervene, only to get himself killed for his efforts? Or was there no connection between the two deaths at all?

If Nong Noi and Banditto had been killed on the same night, the killer could have hidden Banditto's body in the death room, while leaving Nong Noi's body in a place where it would certainly be found. He could have gouged out Noi's eyes to make certain the body was covered by a sheet. Then, when Nong Noi's body was taken to the death room to be prepared for the funeral rites, he could have switched them, stuffing Nong Noi's body in the top slot of the crematorium, knowing we would use the bottom, while sealing up Banditto in Noi's coffin.

But who had access to the death room? Brother Suchinno and his assistants. Who had prepared Nong Noi's body for the rites? Brother Suchinno and his assistants. They prepared all bodies for cremation. Was Suchinno the killer we were searching for? He was not well educated, but a hard worker and handy with tools. He didn't strike me as the murdering kind. Then again, how could I be sure? What did I know about the man, really?

If it had been Brother Suchinno, he could have easily switched the bodies, and he would have known exactly which slot would be used for the cremation, and when. It was his job to fire the oven, and then to collect the ashes afterward. In this case, there would have been far too much ash on the tray, but he could have easily concealed it, and none of us would have been any the wiser.

If Suchinno had killed the boy, then perhaps Banditto saw him and threatened to turn him in. Perhaps Suchinno had no choice but to kill him too.

And yet it was hard to believe Suchinno was capable of such a thing. Not impossible, but extremely difficult. Suchinno was much too good-hearted, much too simple of a man to be involved with such things.

If my suspicions were correct, then Chao's "monks" were running a drug business, perhaps using our boys to make deliveries. Had Nong Noi gotten himself mixed with up these bogus monks? Did Nong Noi kill Banditto then got himself killed for his trouble?

I thought about Brother Satchapalo. The syringe had been found outside of his kuti, and although a search of his kuti revealed nothing, it had been Chao and his men who had conducted the search — if Chao was in on it, he would have protected Satchapalo and said nothing had been found.

The attack with the snake also presented problems. How was it done? How did one smuggle such a creature into the monastery complex without anyone noticing? Where was it kept? I was not willing to believe that it was simply coincidence — that a cobra had found its way to the monastery grounds and just happened to find its way to my kuti.

How did our killer get his hands on a cobra? A monk couldn't simply get on a bus and go to a pet store and purchase a venomous snake. At the Chatuchuk Market, perhaps. And even if he found such a place, he couldn't carry it on a bus. And even if he could, he wouldn't have been able to bring it into the monastery without a lot of questions being asked. And how was he going to get the money for it anyway?

But if you were a rich man — as Chao was — with access to a variety of businesses, resorts and plantations, all over the country, then perhaps it was not hard at all. And after I had rattled his cage, was it any surprise that he wanted me out of the way?

I tried a new line of thought: What facts did I have at my disposal?

There was the fact that two people were now dead. Someone had made an attempt on my life. There was a drug business going on at the temple.

For evidence, I had a bloodied tank top and a pair of shorts, crumpled up newspaper that yielded no fingerprints, and a Buddhist medal found in the bottom of the water jar where one of the victims had been dumped. That medal was made by an abbot in Ubon Ratchathani.

I had two victims: One was found nude, the other found wearing a sarong. This suggested their deaths occurred at night.

No matter how I tried to put the facts together to formulate a workable theory, I didn't seem to be any closer to the truth than when I had started.

Four

I was prodded awake the next morning by an insistent hand. I opened my eyes.

Brother Satchapalo was standing by my bed, looking at me strangely.

Alarm bells went off.

It was early morning. I heard the shower going in the bathroom. Jak was nowhere to be seen.

"Are you looking for your crippled kuti boy?" Satchapalo asked, sneering.

My heart began to race in my chest.

"He's taking a shower," Satchapalo said.

"What do you want?" I asked, hardly enough air in my lungs to get the words out.

"I brought you a candle from my boss," he said, smiling, pulling a fat, yellow candle out of the pocket in his orange robe. "He said I needed to make amends for screwing up with the snake. Nothing personal, Ananda. It's just you should be more respectful, you know? The boss doesn't like your attitude."

And then, with an astonishing speed, he darted forward, catching me by the jaw and forcing my mouth open with one hand, the other holding the candle that he shoved into my mouth and pushed down on.

I convulsed, tried to get air, choking, terrified, half-fogged with sleep and disbelief.

His fingers pinched my nostrils shut, cutting off any air I might have gotten.

He grinned, showing me tobacco-stained teeth, and then suddenly relented, removing his fingers from my nose, allowing me to take a desperate breath.

"Boss said I had to bring your eyes, so he would know you were dead," he whispered, bending close to me, putting his thumb over my right eye and pushing down on it, as if teasing me. "You see, Ananda, if you just push down, like that, and you keep pushing, you can poke your thumb all the way through to the brain. Did you know that?"

I was in such a state that my bladder let go, wetting my hospital robe and the thin covering, but I hardly noticed it.

He squeezed my nostrils shut again, leering at me, letting me know that he was enjoying my suffering.

I lurched on the bed, trying to get away from him, but he was young and strong and I was old and not in the best of health. His fingers and hands were like iron, bearing down on me with incredible force. I twisted my body this way and that.

My efforts were futile.

Was this what Nong Noi had endured during his last moments? Had he been woken, a candle shoved down his throat, his oxygen supply cut off? Had he struggled just as vainly? Had his eyes already been gouged out, or did that come afterward?

I was gagging, frantic, pulling at Satchapalo's arms with all my strength, jerking my body on the bed, desperate to get away from him, to get air, desperate to live, to keep on living.

Satchapalo was the killer!

But why?

There was sharp pain in my jaw and cheeks — he was bearing down on the candle so hard I thought he just might break my jaw and tear it right off my face. My teeth were digging into the yellow wax of the candle, the taste of it sickening.

It reminded me of how Nong Noi's teeth had been stuck on the wax of the candle that had been shoved down his throat.

I tried to keep my eyes open, but I was having trouble. I tried to wrench my body away, but there was no strength in my limbs. I tried to use my fingernails to tear at his arms, but he shrugged it off. I was too weak to do anything to stop him. He grinned, hunched over me, his eyes full of excitement.

Was it time to die now? Had I been given a few days' grace to prepare for the real thing? Was it just a matter now of fading into that blackness and forgetfulness and moving on to whatever might lay ahead in the next life? Had I done the best I could with this current life?

I didn't want to die.

Satchapalo's face was hard, all angles and lines. The muscles on his arms were straining, bulging. His eyes were dark slits. He had acted with the cool professionalism of a man who had done this before, maybe many times before.

How long would it take to kill me? A minute? My kuti boy, in the shower, wouldn't hear a thing. Neither would the nurses outside at their receptionist's desk. No one would hear a thing. What could I do but flop around the bed like a fish taken from a net and thrown onto a wooden dock?

I didn't want to die!

There was a commotion then, shrieking, a flash of bare skin — my kuti boy. He attacked Satchapalo from behind, using a metal pitcher that still had water in it — it was leaking out and flying every which way as he swung it at the back of Satchapalo's head.

Satchapalo let go of me, backed away, surprised.

Jak was screaming, an eerie howling sort of grief and fright. But suddenly he stopped — Satchapalo whirled and backhanded him. His small body was thrown against the edge of the television stand. He struck his head on the wood and fell down, the pitcher clattering to the floor.

He did not get up.

Satchapalo glared at me, as if trying to decide whether he should risk finishing the job. There was a commotion outside – the nurses had heard Jak scream. Satchapalo bared his teeth. "You'll die another day, holy man," he snarled, before racing out of the room.

I took in a breath through my nose, trying to bring my hands up to take the candle out of my mouth. I was shaking. I was completely terrified.

Nurses ran into the room, shouting.

Five

I woke later that day and couldn't speak. My mouth, jaw and throat were in such pain I could hardly swallow. I was grateful just to lie there.

"Don't try to speak, Ananda."

The abbot sat down on my bed and regarded me for long moments.

"You scared us all to death," he said, chuckling. "I don't think there's anything for you to worry about now."

I didn't think this was so, but it hurt too much to talk, so I merely nodded.

"Satchapalo was the killer, wasn't he?" he asked.

It certainly looked that way. There was no way to prove he had killed Nong Noi or Brother Banditto, but in attacking me — and perhaps being unexpectedly thwarted by my kuti boy — he had given himself away.

"We were rolled," the abbot said, looking dejected. "I've been doing a bit of investigating myself. Chao doesn't run any undercover operation — he's in the training department, and all he does is train officers in forensic techniques. It was Kittisaro, actually, that helped me to figure it out."

Kittisaro?

"You asked him to look up gouged out eyes on the Internet, to see what he could find. He found something, just like he told you. Maybe Chao himself runs this gang. Maybe he puts his men undercover at monasteries, where they can have access to kids who make the deliveries for them. I don't know all the details, Ananda, but I've turned over all the information I have to Lt. Somchai, and the police are looking into it. Anyway, I don't think they'll be bothering us anymore."

We sat in silence. I wanted to speak, to ask questions, but I just sat there and waited for him to continue.

"You were lucky," he said at last, giving me a small smile. "If your kuti boy had come out of that bathroom twenty to thirty seconds after he did, I'd be offering chants for you right about now and you'd be lying in a coffin listening to us. He saved your life, that boy did."

I nodded. He had indeed.

"Now listen, Ananda. I'm talking now as your abbot, your superior. You keep yourself in this bed. You're going to rest for a few days. You look like hell. You're going to give yourself time to heal and get better. I'm leaving Brother Suchinno here, with his assistants — Chittasangwaro and Salisangwaro. We've got the staff on standby, looking out for anyone who looks suspicious or wants to know where your room is. I can't take much more of this."

"Where's Jak?" I whispered.

"Ananda ..."

"Where?" I asked. My throat was raw and the word was like broken glass scraping across the insides of my mouth.

The abbot frowned, and alarm bells began ringing in my mind. "He's not doing so well, Ananda. He's in the children's ward. He sustained a serious injury when he hit his head on that television stand."

"How bad?" I managed to ask.

The abbot frowned again. "He's in a coma."

I sat up in my bed and began picking at the IV, which had been inserted on the back of my left hand.

"What are you doing?" the abbot demanded.

"Have to see him," I rasped.

I did. For some reason — I wasn't thinking clearly — I had to see him. I had to know he was alive. I had to be there for him, even if all I could do was watch him die.

"Ananda, lie down," the abbot ordered.

I ignored him, swinging my legs out of the bed. My head felt strange as the blood rushed around. I was weak. I was afraid I wouldn't be able to stand up at all. But I had to see that boy.

Brother Suchinno was at my side, pushing me down, trying to restrain me.

"Ananda!" the abbot exclaimed. "Really! You're in no condition to go anywhere. Be reasonable. There's nothing you can do for the boy."

"Maybe we could get a wheelchair," Suchinno suggested.

I nodded.

The abbot was flustered. "Well if you promise to lie there and give us two minutes, we'll take you over there."

I lay back on the pillow, wincing — I had caused myself to hurt in places I didn't know I had been injured in.

Brother Suchinno came back to the room with a nurse and a wheelchair, and they helped me to get out of bed and sit down on it.

"You're going to be nothing but trouble, aren't you?" the nurse asked, smiling broadly, suggesting he knew exactly how to deal with the likes of me — which he probably did.

We got onto an elevator, went to another floor, down many corridors and through various lobbies until at last we went through a set of large double doors, the entrance to the poor ward, where sixteen beds were lined up, separated by white curtains.

Jak's bed was all the way at the end, by the window.

He was lying on the bed, attached to a breathing device, various wires taped to his bare chest and arms, an IV attached to his left hand, looking somehow small and insignificant under a thin covering.

"His brain is swelling," the nurse said quietly as I took Jak's hand into my own and stared at him. "Filling up with blood. It's just a matter of time."

"Operation?" I whispered, looking up to the abbot.

"Ananda, there's no money for that," he said.

"No money?" I asked.

He was embarrassed, took his eyes away.

"It would be very expensive," the male nurse said, as if to rescue him. "And the boy has no insurance, and the hospital doesn't have funds to cover it. It happens. The best we can do is to keep him comfortable."

He said this the way one would expect him to do so, with professional detachment, just stating the facts.

"Perhaps that's the best *you* can do," I said angrily.

I wasn't about to let this boy die, and I thought I knew a way to save him.

Six

Jentara came in to my room hesitantly, perfectly aware of the rules of etiquette — that a woman shouldn't be anywhere near a monk, much less at his bedside. But sometimes the rules have to be broken.

Suchinno had given me a pad of paper with a pen. He now stood on the other side of the bed, acting as a chaperone, of sorts.

I wrote: *You want your story?*

She looked at me and smiled.

One condition. My kuti boy. Take his picture. Mention there's no money for an operation. Tomorrow's paper. Front page. Possible?

She nodded.

It was a painfully long time before I could write down everything I wanted to tell her — about Chao and his men, about Nong Noi's death, about the snake in my kuti and the subsequent attack while I was recovering, about the drug operation that I suspected was being run. I told her everything I could think of. Let her make of it what she would.

She summoned a photographer, who took my picture, and then Jak's.

When she was finished, I settled back in the bed and hoped it would be enough.

Seven

"Not your best picture," Brother Suchinno said the following morning, handing me a copy of Thai Rath.

My picture was in a corner on the front page. "MONK AND BOY ATTACKED AT HOSPITAL BY DRUG GANG," the headline screamed. Another picture, the inset, showed Jak lying on his bed, eyes closed, clinging to a life that was slowly ebbing away.

Suchinno was right. I looked like someone had beaten me to within an inch of my life. There were dark circles under my eyes and I looked haggard and old.

I read the story, surprised by Jentara's tact and professionalism. In the third paragraph she mentioned that Jak was going to die unless money could be found for an operation to relieve the pressure on his swelling brain.

Throughout the article, she was careful about names, and made heavy use of words like "alleged" and "reportedly." It would put a lot of pressure on Chao. Furthermore, she had included mug shots of Chao's four "monks," which she had taken from their files. That would keep the men on the run for quite some time.

While I was reading, the nurse strolled in, offering a grin. "You've got the right sort of friends, I see, power of the press and all of that. The operators at the switchboard have been fielding calls all morning. If we're lucky, we might come up with enough money for that boy's operation."

I smiled.

"If we're lucky," he said, as if he didn't want me to get too comfortable. "Now. Do we need the bedpan, or a trip to the bathroom?"

Eight

Later that evening, Suchinno wheeled me to Jak's room, and we sat with him for almost an hour. I held his hand. No words were said.

I thought about what the Lord Buddha taught his disciples, that nothing lasts forever, that we are all in a state of flux, of constant change, changing even from moment to moment. We are born, we age, we get sick, and then we die. There is somehow an unsatisfactoriness about this whole business.

"There is suffering," the Buddha had said simply. Not that everything about life was suffering, but rather the simple fact that suffering existed, that there was suffering.

We cling to life, knowing it cannot last. We refuse the inevitable. We watch others die, but never think that one day it will be our turn — or that of a loved one.

Jak was motionless. The thin covering had been pulled up to his waist, leaving his upper body exposed — this being the poor ward, it was rather warm. His chest rose and fell slowly. His skin had the blush of youth and vitality. His dark hair spilled about the pillow. A large bandage was on the side of his face, near the temple on the left side, where he had struck the corner of the television stand.

The way he laid there, not speaking, not moving, unaware of our presence, an air hose down his throat, reminded me of how fragile we are, how easy it is for us to die.

The thought of death ought not to be depressing. It's only a fact of life. A proper appreciation for this fact can lead to greater appreciation of life, for whatever days remain to us. When we see life slipping away from someone we love, we are reminded that our own days are numbered, that none of us will live forever, that we too will follow.

As Buddhists, we take comfort in the idea that this life isn't all there is, that another life awaits, another chance to do it all over again. We make as much merit as we can, hoping these good deeds will follow us into that next life, that conditions there might be better, that we might be in a better position to practice the Lord Buddha's teachings, and move further along the path to enlightenment.

Although there is pain in parting, we know that our loved ones have gone on ahead, and will take another rebirth, and that we will most likely see them again. In this life we might have been brother and sister. In the next life we might be father and daughter, or husband and wife.

"We should go, Ananda," Suchinno said, moving to stand behind me, putting his hand on my shoulder.

I wanted to cry — I wanted the release of it, the way it cleansed and somehow made everything seem better. But I could not cry. That part of me was broken.

I was trying to prepare myself for the death of this boy, trying to be philosophical, to retreat into Buddhist thought, to give up hope, to let things be as they would be. It wasn't for me to decide whether this boy lived or not. Even if we could get him an operation, there were no guarantees.

Yet I couldn't help believing that we had been thrown together for a reason, that he had something to teach me, and I had something to teach him.

Had the chance come and gone already?

"Come on," Suchinno said.

He wheeled me back to my room, where we discovered a visitor — about two dozen, in fact. Suchinno was confused. I was, too. The visitors congregated at the door to my room, and when they saw us coming they moved out of the way respectfully, and a tall, elegant woman stepped forward and offered a wai of respect.

"Father Ananda?" she said.

I was so bewildered that I let myself look at her for a long moment before remembering that I wasn't supposed to do any such thing. But she was simply stunning.

I nodded my head.

"Don't try to talk," she said kindly. "I know your throat is ... well, anyway, don't say anything. My name is Supatra. I'm an actress. Maybe you've seen me? I wanted you to know I read about you in the newspaper and I want to pay for that boy's operation. I don't care what it costs. It doesn't matter to me. That boy deserves to live, and if this hospital thinks they're going to let him die because they can't afford to operate on him, well, they have another thing coming, don't they? And my friends and I also want to fund your youth program over there at Wat Mahanat. I want you to help those boys, Father Ananda. Who needs that Chao fellow? I came here to tell you this so you wouldn't be worried about it while you're recovering. I do hope you'll get better soon."

I was so surprised I couldn't speak.

"He's not well," Suchinno said. "But of course we're very grateful. We could show you to the boy's room, if you like."

She nodded, and then bent down on one knee and asked me to bless her.

I did my best, whispering the words, trying hard to remember what they were.

Brother Chittasangwaro and Brother Salisangwaro, both looking sheepish, emerged from my room. Brother Chittasangwaro took me in hand while Suchinno and Salisangwaro led the actress and her entourage away.

Chittasangwaro helped me get into the bed.

"Do you know who that was?" he asked, his eyes wide with amazement.

I shook my head. I hadn't watched television in years.

He laughed, informing me that our new patroness was a well-known television soap opera star — and heir to the enormous fortune her parents had made in the construction business.

Whoever she was, I was grateful, and after Chittasangwaro got me settled in bed, I fell asleep and slept for a long time.

CHAPTER SEVEN

"But whosoever in this world overcomes this wretched craving so difficult to overcome, his sorrows fall away from him like water-drops from a lotus (leaf)."

The Lord Buddha. From the Dhammapada, #336.

One

"If I didn't know better, I'd say you were becoming a sentimental old fool," Suchinno said.

"I can't help it," I said miserably.

"I know that," he replied. "And I'm not saying you should, either. You might try to stop blaming yourself."

"But it was my fault!" I said rather too forcefully. My throat seized up in pain, as if to protest.

Jak had been taken into surgery about an hour ago, and we were waiting. I was beside myself with worry. I was tired and lying in bed, and yet felt guilty for lying in bed and wanted to get up. But get up and do what?

"I could have one of the brothers bring along my oilcan and we'll take care of that squeak in your voice," Suchinno said.

I wanted to respond to his humor, but I couldn't. I was too busy being wretchedly self-involved.

"Well, if it was your fault, then it was my fault too, Ananda," he said. He was sitting on the edge of my bed, regarding me with patient eyes. "You see," he said, "I was going to come to the hospital that morning when you were attacked, but I didn't. But if I had, I could have prevented everything. So it's all my fault."

"Stop it," I said, annoyed.

"Just trying to make you see how ridiculous you sound," he replied, shrugging.

He was right, of course.

"Don't you have any toasters to fix?" I asked.

"Lots of them," he said. "But they're not going anywhere, are they?"

I was in no condition to be having a conversation.

"He's going to be fine," Suchinno said. "Why don't you try to sleep? All this fretting isn't going to help anything."

The operation was going to take anywhere from two to six hours, and the nurse had promised he would come when there was any information to convey.

I fell into a light, restless sleep, waking up every now and again expecting to see the doctor standing by my bed, but finding only Suchinno, or Chittasangwaro, or Salisangwaro.

It was going to be a long afternoon.

Two

It *was* my fault.

Jak had been so keen on staying with me, on helping me, on just being there because I was sick and in need, and I had allowed it. I could have sent him back to the monastery, back to the care of Brother Khantiphalo and the homeless youth program, where he would have been safe. I could have requested that one of the monks come to the hospital and tend to my needs, as Suchinno and his assistants were now doing. But I hadn't the heart to send Jak away, because I knew he was proud to be able to take care of me, to be of some use to me, happy to feel needed.

Kids were that way. The worse thing you could do to them was make them feel you had no use for them, that their presence didn't matter one way or the other, that they had nothing they could possibly offer you.

So I had let him stay.

Of course I had no way of knowing how it would turn out. And the boy had saved my life. Who's to say the same would have happened had one of the monks been there? It could have all turned out rather differently.

It was now four hours after the surgery had begun, and we still hadn't received word.

Just as I was getting ready to ask Suchinno to go check and see what was happening, the door to my room opened and the male nurse strolled in.

"He's out now," he said quietly. "He's stable. The operation was successful, but he's not out of the woods yet. But he's made it this far and that's a very good sign."

"Can we see him?" I asked.

He shook her head. "No, I'm afraid you can't. Perhaps tomorrow. And please remember it could be days before he comes around — it could be a long wait. And while surgeries like this are generally successful, once the patient makes it this far, still, there are no guarantees. It can go either way."

He was telling us what he had to tell us, warning us not to get our hopes up too high, that there was still risk. But at least he had made it this far, and that was something.

"He's a strong kid," Suchinno said, standing at the foot of my bed and looking at me. "You just wait and see."

Three

The days went by slowly, and I began to recover.

Jak did not wake up. He was stable, resting well, and apparently doing well. He just wasn't waking up.

Lt. Somchai had visited to give me a progress report, which consisted of his saying there was basically no progress to report, that Chao and his men were nowhere to be found. He was ready to conclude that Satchapalo had been Nong Noi's killer and had also, for reasons known only to him, killed Banditto.

I wasn't ready to draw any conclusions yet.

Jentara fed a steady stream of stories and photos to her newspaper, and the publicity it was generating was hard to fathom. While well-wishers sent me numerous flowers and cards, they were nothing compared to the flowers and cards piling up for Jak to see — when he eventually woke up. The involvement of Supatra, his high-profile celebrity profile, had made him something of a celebrity himself, and the nurses passed on the complaint from the switchboard that so many people were calling to ask how he was doing that the switchboard operators couldn't get any work done.

It would be good for him to know that so many people cared about him.

After eight days in the hospital, I was ready to leave.

Suchinno helped me to dress one final time. He had become like my mother.

"I'd like to see Jak before we leave," I said.

Suchinno nodded. Chittasangwaro and Salisangwaro gathered up our things, Suchinno produced a wheelchair, and soon we were all at Jak's bedside.

All he did was lay in bed. Occasionally, over these past two days, he would moan quietly in his sleep or move his head from side to side, which the nurses said were very good signs that he was coming around.

Still, I was heartsick.

I took his hand into my own. "We're going to leave now, little brother. But we'll come visit every day. All you have to do is get better."

I whispered the words, afraid someone would hear them.

His face was obscured by the bandaging that was wrapped all the way around his head, and he did not answer.

I was embarrassed by the emotion that swelled within me – raw, powerful emotion, of the sort I had not felt in many years, as if my heart had suddenly softened into some sort of sentimental goo.

I was a monk, was I not? How foolish to be at the mercy of intense emotions, to be swept about like a tiny craft on the waves of a roaring sea.

Of course, I knew precisely what was wrong with me, but I was not yet ready to admit it.

Four

We took a taxi back to the monastery.

Throughout my recovery, Khun Charn's words had kept coming back to me: "Follow the leads, Ananda. Follow the leads. The rest is just distraction."

He was absolutely right. If I had done that, I would have figured out the whole thing much faster. There was still time to correct my mistakes.

Contrary to what the abbot so desperately wanted to believe, I knew the case was not yet closed. Chao's men had disappeared, it was true. Chao himself was suddenly unreachable. It did indeed seem as if Satchapalo had been the killer, that he had killed Nong Noi the same way he had tried to kill me.

But some things were bothering me.

Everything had happened too quickly. There were too many clues, too many leads to follow up, still so much patient grunt work to be done, and only the doing of that work would satisfy me as to what had really happened.

Two things, in particular, had captured my interest. Firstly, Jak and I had checked Satchapalo's shoes. He'd had two pairs sitting in front of his kuti, and we had looked at both of them that day when we had gone around checking shoes. Neither matched the footprints in the photographs. Of course, he might have had another pair of shoes that we had not seen. He might have been wearing someone else's, for that matter. But it had not been his shoes in that bathroom, that night, and that spoke very strongly about whether he had killed Nong Noi — or not.

Secondly, the killer we were looking for had dropped a medal at the crime scene — a medal made in Ubon Ratchathani. Satchapalo and the others were from the North, and did not, as far as I could recollect, wear Buddhist medals or have any interest in them. Neither, I suspected, had Nong Noi.

I had said nothing of this to the abbot, afraid he would ground me, or force me to give up the search. I was determined to know the truth about Nong Noi's death, and I knew that when I figured it out, it would also explain what had happened to Brother Banditto.

The two deaths were connected. They had happened on the same night. I was willing to bet that whoever had killed Nong Noi was accosted by Banditto, and the killer had no choice but to kill Banditto as well.

It did not, I suspect, have anything to do with drugs or Chao's men.

Nong Noi's death was a crime of passion. Banditto's death had been a necessary afterthought.

Nong Noi was a boy of questionable morals, a nuisance, someone who was disliked, someone who had fallen through the cracks of our society. He was desperate for love and attention, but so full of hurt and anger he had driven everyone away. He no doubt offered the only thing he had — his body — in exchange for the attention and kindness he longed for, even to the point of throwing himself at others.

There would be no points to score in solving his death, no monetary rewards, no grateful relatives. I wouldn't receive any medals for my dogged determination. But his death deserved a proper investigation. It was the very last thing that anyone could do for such a person, at least in this life, and I was determined to do it.

Five

"I need to look through the file on the brothers," I said.

"Father Ananda! Nice to see you. I'm fine, thanks for asking. Are you feeling better?" Kittisaro pulled himself away from his computer and gave me a good long look.

I offered him a small smile, but I was in no mood to be sociable. "Still alive, I guess, Kittisaro. Throat's still a bit sore, but then it would be, wouldn't it?"

"Now what is this about files?" he asked.

"I need to look through them, preferably when the abbot's not in there."

"It seems to me the abbot wouldn't want you doing that. You're supposed to be resting. I'm not supposed to be helping you — that's what the abbot told me."

"And you wouldn't be," I said. "You can go about your lunar thing. Just let me in his office, eh?"

"Can I ask why?"

"You can," I said. "I may not answer. Probably won't. Just need to check a few things and satisfy myself about a few points."

"Uh huh. That's what I thought. Well, he's not in there now, and if you hurry, you might finish before he comes back."

"Where is he?"

"He went out to bless a house."

"So he won't be back for hours?"

"I didn't tell you that," Kittisaro said.

He let me into the abbot's office. He even wanted to help.

"What are you looking for, Father Ananda? I can help. Come on. I won't tell anyone."

I could use his help — the thought of going through all the files, of being on my feet for that long — was not very welcome. I was feeling better, but not that better.

"I'm looking for Ubon Ratchathani. It seems to me that I saw that name in one of these files — someone from Ubon Ratchathani."

"What's so significant about that?" Kittisaro asked.

"I found a Buddhist medal at the crime scene. It was made by an abbot at a temple in Ubon Ratchathani. I think the killer may have dropped it."

Kittisaro whistled.

"I think it's in the P's," I said, going to the middle of the filing cabinets and starting there.

"I'll start next to you in the M's and work my way back down. How about that?"

I nodded.

One by one I looked through the files, skipping those for deceased monks. We worked steadily for almost an hour, Kittisaro every so often running off to answer the phone in front or tend to business.

I got all the way to the end of my side, with no luck.

Most of our monks had come from Bangkok and its surrounding areas.

Kittisaro got down to the C's. He handed me the large stack of them and moved over to the A's and B's.

I put the files down on top of the cabinet in front of me, closing my eyes.

"I know who it is," I said. I could remember now, quite clearly, looking at this brother's file. "It's Chittakhutto. You gave me his file that day, and I looked through it. Chittakhutto's the one from Ubon Ratchathani. Why didn't I think of that earlier?"

Chittkhutto was the would-be scholar who was up for a royal title – exactly the sort of monk who would be a big fan of Buddhist medallions.

I opened my eyes and glanced over at Kittisaro.

"Are you listening to me?" I asked.

He was not. He was looking at a file full of clippings about a double murder that had happened eight years ago. A woman and her son had been gunned down, execution style, by a drug gang in front of their small home in a Bangkok inner city suburb. There was a picture of a boy sitting in the front of a truck, a bullet hole in his head, with another picture of a woman lying on the ground, shot dead, blood pooling around her body.

Kittisar glanced at me, aghast. "This is your file," he said quietly. "This is what happened to your wife and your son, isn't it? Ananda, why didn't you tell me?"

He held up one of the clippings showing the photo of the dead boy.

My son.

Suthipong.

The sight of him made it hard to breathe.

It all came back to me in a rush of feelings and emotions.

For eight years I had been running away from what some photographer had so clumsily captured on a piece of film, and which some newspaper had printed on its front page. Not a day had gone by that I hadn't blamed myself for my son's death, for my wife's death, for the suffering I had caused both of them. It was that one thing in my life that I could not bring myself to accept.

"I'm sorry, Ananda," Kittisaro said. "I didn't know."

I did not answer, could not answer.

The grief was potent.

I had run from this grief all these years. It threatened to overwhelm me, crush me, destroy me. No amount of Buddhist mediation or practice could make it go away.

"I need to sit down," I said, my voice choked.

Six

I was the sum total of my experiences — that was all any person could be, really. All of my life's experiences, the good, the bad, the pleasurable, the painful, they all combined to form this person that I thought of as myself, as being my "self." To reject any part of that experience was to invite disharmony, affliction, suffering, mental anguish.

I had done just that. Continued to do it. All the bits of my life could be accepted with the exception of one — that day I had come home from work and discovered the bodies of my wife and son.

At the time, I was a police officer and had just been switched to the anti-narcotics division. We had scored a big hit, having been tipped off as to a suspected drug warehouse. We raided it, came away with three suspects and 20,000 speed pills — a huge haul in those days. There was a picture in Thai Rath the next day of all those pills lying on a table in front of the handcuffed suspects, with the police officers involved, myself included, standing in the background.

It was a proud moment for us. We had hurt the bad guys. We had taken some of the pills off the streets. We were making a difference.

The day after that picture appeared in Thai Rath, I went home and found my wife's body lying the street by the gate to our small house, with my son's body still in the car — my wife had gotten out of the Toyota and was opening the gate, after fetching him from school, when a motorcyclist with a gunman riding the back drove up and parked.

She was thirty-eight. He was thirteen. After him, we had not been able to have any more children, though we had tried.

The killings had been carried out execution style, not more than five minutes before I had arrived.

We hit them. They hit us.

After the funeral rites for my wife and son, I quit the police department and joined the monkhood, not intending to stay, just hoping for a way to learn to cope with my grief.

Eight years had gone by.

Sooner or later I was going to have to forgive myself for what I had not been able to prevent that day.

Seven

It took me awhile to get hold of myself.

"I have what I need," I said at last, opening my eyes, and looking at Kittisaro. "But I need some more help from you. Can you show me the sign-out sheets for the day after Nong Noi's murder?"

He gave me a puzzled look. "Sure," he said, going to his desk and picking up a clipboard, fumbling through several sheets until he found the right day. "Are you alright?" he asked, his face a mask of concern.

"Kittisaro, that happened eight years ago. Stop looking at me like that."

He lowered his eyes.

"Did Brother Chittakhutto sign out on that day?" I asked.

He looked, nodded.

"In the afternoon?" I asked.

"About 2:30 p.m."

"Where's my case file for Nong Noi's death?"

"The abbot took it."

"I need it."

"Ananda-"

"Just get it, Kittisaro . If he's angry about it, send him to me."

Kittisaro sighed, went to the abbot's office and retrieved the file.

Inside were the photographs that Lt. Somchai's men had taken of the footprints in the bathroom where Nong Noi had been found. I took these out, and gave the file back to Kittisaro.

I then looked at Chittakhutto's file. He was an excellent student. In fact, we had no one smarter, no one brighter, no one with more certificates and degrees and testimonies as to his academic excellence. He was on the career ladder, heading up the Buddhist hierarchy. His work was so impressive he was being considered for a royal title.

He had a lot to lose, in other words, if a boy like Nong Noi spread word around that Chittakhutto had broken his vows, had perhaps engaged in sexual intercourse with a homeless boy, perhaps even had a relationship with such a boy.

He had been worried that day, when I had interviewed him, over the matter of whether he had broken his vows. He would know, of course, that if he had broken his vows in that fashion, he would be instantly defrocked, that all his certificates and degrees would mean nothing in the face of it — and his hopes for promotion and appointments and titles would be destroyed. That would give him a rather powerful motive to shut Nong Noi up. For good.

"Kittisaro, can you call Lt. Somchai at the Silom Police Station and ask him to come over right away, and bring some men? He's going to need to make an arrest."

Wordless, he nodded.

"Now, can you call Brother Suchinno and tell him to come over here? Tell him to bring a large wrench and a syringe."

"A wrench? A syringe?"

"Just do it," I said.

Kittisaro grabbed up the phone.

A minute later Suchinno appeared at the door. "Would you like to tell me what's going on?" he asked. He handed me a syringe. Holding up the wrench, he said, "What am I supposed to do with this?"

"We're going to catch a killer."

I turned back to Kittisaro. "One more thing. Can you ring the emergency bell so that all of the brothers will gather in the main sala? After about ten minutes, I want you to send someone over there to say it was just a false alarm, a mistake. Okay? But don't do it too soon. I need at least ten minutes."

He was now beyond questioning me, and simply did as I asked.

The bell went off. It was not used often, but everyone knew what it meant, and what they were supposed to do when they heard it.

"Shall we?" I said to Suchinno.

He smiled.

We walked to the main sala, and positioned ourselves off to one side where we could watch the brothers as they arrived.

"What are we waiting for?" Suchinno asked.

"You'll see in a minute," I said.

The brothers gathered quickly, glancing at us, perplexed, removing their shoes at the entrance and padding inside on bare feet.

I waited for Brother Chittakhutto to appear.

He did.

Like the other monks, he left his shoes near the entryway, and he went into the prayer hall and sat down in his customary place.

I walked over to the maze of shoes, picked up one of Chittakhutto's, looking at the bottom. The tread matched exactly the prints in the bathroom that Lt. Somchai's men had photographed.

"Do you mind telling me what we're doing?" Suchinno asked, looking at me as if I had gone a bit crackers.

"I wanted some proof, and I've got it," I said. "We've got some work to do."

Together we began walking through the complex, heading to the kutis.

"What work is that?" Suchinno asked.

"We need to have a look at something."

EIGHT

I was never going to be a stand-in for James Bond, with nerves of steel and a genius for getting myself out of complicated — deadly — situations. The state of my nerves was roughly equivalent to that of a cat in room full of rocking chairs and old folks. I was, after all, just an aging monk a bit out of his depth.

We went to Chittakhutto's kuti.

"You stay outside and keep watch," I said. "I don't want any else attacking me. When you see Chittakhutto coming, knock on the window, get my attention. I won't be long. Whatever you do, don't let him see you. And keep that wrench handy in case you need to whack him over the head. And grab his shoes."

I was trembling when I walked up the steps to Chittakhutto's kuti and went inside. What did I expect to find anyway — the proverbial smoking gun? Another dead body? A signed confession?

I took a deep breath, trying to relax my nerves. I might not find anything at all. But I had to try.

Chittakhutto had rather unhelpfully opened his drapes, and the sunlight was shining through the windows — and leaving me exposed to view to anyone who might walk by.

To my left was a small bed, a mattress lying on the floor. The bed had been neatly made up. A large fan was positioned close to it, which was plugged into the kuti's only electricity outlet. To my right was a series of small book shelves, each housing numerous titles, stacked in no particular fashion. Chittakhutto was an avid reader. Around the bookcases, on the floor, were stacks of papers and magazines, most dealing with Buddhist medals, of which he seemed to be fond — there was a small stack of them by the magazines, still in their small plastic boxes.

One of those plastic boxes would be empty, I suspected.

To the right side of the front door was a hamper for dirty clothes; to the left was a plastic container, the rectangular sort used to store items, containing a set of orange robes and what few clothes Chittakhutto possessed — two pairs of white socks, an old pair of shorts, a heavy T-shirt.

I got down on my hands and knees and began searching, lifting up the edges of the mattress to see if anything had been hidden beneath the bed, looking through the bookcases, behind the books, through the papers and magazines, through the plastic container full of clothes, even through his dirty clothes hamper and waste paper basket. I found nothing out of the ordinary, nothing that would link him definitively to the murders.

I was sweating. My nerves were on edge, expecting, at any moment, for the door to fly open and Chittakhutto to discover me hunched over his things.

That was ridiculous, of course. Suchinno was just outside and would give me plenty of warning.

I stood, looking around at the walls, in all the nooks and crannies.

Nothing.

On a whim, I knelt down next to his bed, picking up the pillow. When I was a child, I used to hide things in the pillowcase, thinking no one would ever think to look there. Of course, that was the first place anyone would look, but I didn't know that.

There was nothing.

I went to the small mountain of plastic boxes and began looking through them. One of them had to be empty. It would provide one more piece of evidence.

Where had he gotten so many of these medals?

At last, I was rewarded. I picked up a small box labeled "Ubon Ratchathani." It was empty.

There was a tap on the window.

Startled, I got to my feet, and looked out.

"He's coming," Suchinno whispered.

"Don't let him see you, but stay close," I whispered back. "I need a witness to our conversation."

"But he could be dangerous!"

"No, he's not," I said, rather more bravely than I felt. But I didn't believe he was dangerous at all. In fact, I was quite certain he was a coward.

I positioned myself in the corner of Chittakhutto's kuti near the door, where he wouldn't be likely to see me, and waited.

Nine

The kuti shook a little when Chittakhutto came up the steps and pushed through the door, walking into the middle of the kuti and stopping, looking around, as if he suspected something.

"I've been waiting for you," I said, startling him.

He whirled around and looked at me in complete surprise. His lower lip trembled.

I moved so that I was standing in front of the door. I took the syringe out of the pocket to my robe, and pulled the plastic tip off the needle. I pulled back the plunger, and held the syringe in my hand as if I meant to stab him with it. I did it all very slowly, watching his reaction.

"Is this what you did?" I asked. "Did you learn, in all your studying and reading, that you could kill someone with a syringe full of air, that the air bubbles would get into their veins and cause convulsions and a most painful death?"

He didn't answer.

"Is that how you killed Brother Banditto?" I pressed.

He licked his lips and seemed completely unnerved.

"A cowardly crime, wasn't it? Did you go up behind him, and stab him? Too afraid to face him, man to man, so you stabbed him in the back?"

Chittakhutto wasn't answering, wasn't taking any of the bait I was offering. I needed a confession — and I needed it to be heard by Brother Suchinno, who, I hoped, was just outside and listening through the window.

"What are you doing?" he asked in a shaky voice. "Satchapalo killed that boy. Everyone knows that."

"No he didn't, Chittakhutto, and you know he didn't, because you know who did it. And so do I. I just want to know why. Did you let him sleep with you again, and sometime during the night, cram that candle into his mouth, choking him to death? Is that what happened? You couldn't just kill him. You had to wait until he was vulnerable. And you attacked. Isn't that right?"

He had gone pale. His body was trembling. He had the look of someone who knows he's been caught. He sank to his knees, looking frightened.

"He was the one who came to my room," he said in a shaky voice.

"And then what?"

"It was just like I told you. I made him put his clothes back on. He wanted me to hold him, so I did. We fell asleep."

He lowered his gaze. He seemed to be lost in the memory of that night.

"And then what?" I pressed.

"I woke up," he said, looking up to me and looking down again, as if he was ashamed. "He was doing something to me. I tried to make him stop but I couldn't. I mean, I didn't want him to. I had never felt anything like that. I mean, people talked about it, but I never knew how it felt, what it was like. And I was trying to push him away from me, and something came over me, and it was crazy. And then it was over. And I didn't know what to do, Ananda."

He looked up to me, his eyes pleading.

"And when he came back the next night?"

He shook his head, wouldn't answer.

"So he made you break your vows, didn't he?"

"It wasn't my fault!" he exclaimed hotly. "He was all over me. I was confused."

"So you did it again?" I asked.

He was breathing heavily, grimacing, as if the memory of it was painful.

"And then he threatened to blackmail you, didn't he?"

He looked up to me. "He told me some story about Satchapalo giving him drugs to deliver. I didn't believe him. I mean, he was always talking nonsense. And half the time, he was high. He didn't even know what he was doing himself. I would come back to my kuti and find him lying here, glassy-eyed, high as a kite, lying on my bed like he owned it. What could I do?"

"What did he tell you about Satchapalo?"

Chittakhutto seemed bewildered, as if suddenly his whole life was ending. And in a way, perhaps it was.

"He came to my kuti one night, crying. He showed me some burns on his chest. They had been made with a cigarette. This was after he had stopped coming around, after I had gone to the abbot and forced him to stop. He just came barging in one night, crying, telling me he needed help. He showed me the burns. He was in terrible pain. I made him lie down. He told me Satchapalo had done it because he didn't want Noi leaving their little operation. Satchapalo was getting drugs from somewhere, and then giving them to Noi to deliver. In return, Noi got a steady supply of heroin — that's where I got the syringe. He was always bringing them in here and shooting himself up with them. I couldn't stand it. He said Satchapalo treated him badly, made him do things he didn't want to do, would get him high and ... take advantage. He wanted to get away from the man but he couldn't. He said he had even gone to Thai Rath trying to get Satchapalo exposed but no one would listen to him."

"So he asked you for help?" I said.

"He said if I didn't help him, he was going to expose me. He said he was sick of the hypocrisy of the monks, sick of us do-gooders, sick of us breaking our vows all the time and pretending to be so holy — he went on and on."

"So you had no choice but to kill him?"

He put a hand to his lips, as if to stop the words that wanted to come out.

"So you waited for him to go to sleep, and you got a candle, and you choked him to death, didn't you?"

"He made me break my vows!" Chittakhutto exclaimed, as if that explained everything.

"And he was going to expose you, wasn't he?"

"Yes!"

"So you killed him?"

"Yes! I mean, I didn't mean to. I didn't intend to. I wanted to scare him, make him go away, make him leave me alone. I just wanted him to stop bothering me."

"So when you shoved the candle down his throat, you were just trying to scare him?"

He nodded.

"Why?" I asked.

"I wanted him to stop bothering me! I was sick of him! He was pathetic."

"But then it got out of hand, didn't it, and you wound up killing him?"

Chittakhutto sighed, putting his hands in his lap.

"Banditto saw you, didn't he? Saw you when you were carrying Nong Noi's body to the bathroom, where you dumped it."

"Banditto was laughing at me," he exclaimed, suddenly animated. "Laughing! Said I'd gotten myself mixed up with a two-bit whore and was paying the price for it."

"So you stabbed him?" I asked.

"I don't have to tell you anything," he said quietly, the life going out of him.

"But you do," I said. "You see, Chittakhutto, I already have all the evidence I need. You dropped one of your medals at the crime scene, didn't you? I found it." I showed him the empty plastic box. "I traced it back to your home town, to the abbot of the first monastery you were in, when you first took the robes. If I had to guess, I would say Nong Noi struggled with you, maybe got his hand in your pile of boxes over there and grabbed one of these, not knowing what he was doing. Or maybe you were wearing it that night."

He looked up to me, defeat in his eyes.

"But there's more," I said. "You left your footprints in the bathroom. Your sandals have a distinctive tread mark to them, and they match up exactly with photographs of the footprints we found in the bathroom. So I know you were in the bathroom that night. And you were in there because you were dumping Nong Noi's body in there after you had killed him.

"And that day, when I went around checking shoes, you saw me, and you signed out and you left the monastery, didn't you, because you knew if I saw your shoes, it would be all over. I've got a lot of other evidence," I said, bluffing. "More than enough to satisfy the police. But I just want to clear up a few details, Chittakhutto. I'm trying to fill out the picture of what happened that night."

He was silent for long moments, but then the whole story came pouring out of his mouth. He had waited until Nong Noi fell asleep, and then had choked him. Banditto saw him carrying the body. Made fun of him. Banditto said he would help him, in return for money. Chittakhutto agreed. Banditto told him to disfigure the body, which would confuse the police, and to also put the body in water, which would also confuse the evidence and make it uncertain as to what had happened.

All the while, he was plotting as to how to do away with Banditto. He suggested it would be better to hide the boy's body in the death room, where it would not be discovered for who knew how long. But they had to get in. No problem — Banditto knew how to pick locks. Once he did, Chittakhutto stabbed him with the syringe, wrapped his body in a winding cloth and put it in one of the coffins.

On the day when Nong Noi's body was discovered, he went to the death room at lunchtime, to offer incense sticks. No one else was around. He locked the door. He switched the bodies, leaving Banditto's body to lie in state. He then took the key to the death room and went out to have a copy made and was back before lunch was over.

That night he put Nong Noi's body in the crematorium.

When he finished, he got to his feet, a strange sort of anger in his eyes. He was looking at me, at the syringe in my hand, as if trying to judge whether he had the strength to get it away from me — and use it on me, the way he had used one on Banditto.

"You can't prove anything," he said quietly. "I'm being considered for a royal title! Do you understand what that means to me? Do you know how hard I've worked to get to where I am? Is it money that you want, Ananda? Are you jealous of me? And anyway who cares about that little whore — he was nothing but a heroin addict! Did you expect me to let him stand in my way? Am I supposed to lose everything because of a piece of trash like that?"

He moved forward, his eyes now dark.

"You think you're so smart, don't you, Father Ananda? Such a do-gooder! Sticking your nose in everyone's business. And what are you – just a washed-up has-been who couldn't make it in the real world so you can ran off to a monastery! Pathetic!"

I backed away.

He threw himself at me in a sudden lunge. We fell backwards.

Suchinno raced into the kuti and tore him off me.

I got to my feet, weak with fear.

"You've just made a full confession," I said, "and I wasn't the only one who heard it."

He glared at Suchinno and I.

"The police are on their way. I suggest you get changed, because you're not a monk anymore — you were instantly defrocked, defeated, if not by your sexual involvement with Noi, then with his murder and then the murder of Brother Banditto. Either way, you need to take off those robes and stop pretending to be something you're not."

Ten

Kittisaro knocked on the door to the abbot's office and poked his head inside. "Lt. Somchai's here to see you," he said.

"Show him in," the abbot replied, getting to his feet, as I did.

Lt. Somchai offered us a greeting, which we returned.

"I've got your man in hand," he said. "With the evidence you've supplied, it's pretty much open and shut. He'll be sent away for double murder — you're looking at forty years."

"What about Satchapalo and the others?" I asked.

"We're still looking for them everywhere, but they've gone to ground. It's not likely we'll ever find them, to be honest. Their pictures have been in the papers a lot, though, so maybe one day they'll turn up. They can't hide forever."

"And what about Chao?" I asked.

"Denies any involvement with anything. There's no evidence linking him to any of the crimes."

I figured as much, but I was still disappointed to hear it.

"How's your kuti boy? Any progress yet" he asked.

I shook my head.

"A damned shame," he said quietly. "My men and I will be off now. You've done good work, Father Ananda."

I accompanied him to the parking lot. Chittakhutto sat in the back of their truck, looking lost and small. When he caught sight of me, he flipped me the finger and bared his teeth.

Eleven

Later that evening, I sat on the porch to my kuti. For so long, I had resisted having a kuti boy. Now that I didn't have one, I wanted one.

Yai, one of our boys who ran errands for Kittisaro, came running down the concrete footpath, stopping at the steps to my kuti, looking up at me. "The hospital called, Father Ananda," he exclaimed, breathless. "They said for you to come right away. Kittisaro sent me. I've got money for the taxi."

I was on my feet in an instant. It could be one of two things, and I was hoping against hope that it wasn't what my mind was telling me it was. And yet to be summoned to the hospital could only mean Jak was dying, or perhaps already dead.

"Did they say what happened?" I asked.

"They just said we should go right away."

So we did, flagging down a taxi out front, Yai opening the door for me and giving the driver directions to the hospital.

I reminded myself that hope was all well and good — until it was dashed on the rocks of reality. I would not hope. I would not let myself go down that path. There was no pain worse than that.

The taxi deposited us at the front doors of the hospital, and we made our way inside, but my footsteps slowed and I didn't want to go any further. I guess I just didn't want to know the truth, didn't want to face up to it, and wasn't sure that I could. I sat down in the one of the chairs lining a hall where a variety of people waited to collect their prescriptions from the pharmacy.

Yai crouched down in front of me so that his head would not be higher than mine, giving me a concerned look. "Father Ananda? What is it?"

How could I explain? How could I tell him I couldn't bear the thought of losing someone again? How could I explain to him about my son and my wife? I said nothing, closing my eyes, trying to breathe and steady my nerves.

"Are you sick, father?" Yai asked, sounding bewildered.

I was, but perhaps not in quite the way he meant it.

I did not hear him get up to get one of the nurses walking by.

"Father Ananda?"

I opened my eyes.

Yai was standing beside a young woman, and they were both looking at me oddly.

"Are you sick?" she asked.

I shook my head.

"You must be here to see that boy," she said. "It must be very exciting."

Exciting?

"Is he dying?" I asked quietly, dreading her answer.

"Goodness no, father. He woke up. All the nurses are talking about it. Why don't you go see him?"

The strength suddenly came back to my limbs.

We went to the fifth floor private room where Jak was staying. There was a crowd of nurses and hospital personnel standing outside his door, and they quieted to let us pass.

I went inside and found him sitting on the bed, propped up against pillows, looking very weak and tired, and yet very much alive. He turned when he heard the door open, and gave me a small smile.

I went to his bedside and took his hand and looked at him for long moments, unable to speak, so I said nothing at all.

Yai went to his other side. "You're famous, Jak! Did you know that? Picture in the newspaper and everything! And you've got a movie star paying your bills! We're all waiting for you to get better and come back home."

Home.

I liked the sound of that.

Twelve

The next day, I found myself standing in front of Father Thammarato's kuti.

Each time I saw Nong Noi's dead, defiled body in my mind, I saw my son's dead, defiled body, too – riddled with bullets, blood staining his school uniform, dripping from his mouth, a spasm of pain frozen across his boyish features.

From there my mind jumped to the sight of my wife's body. She lay face down, the back of her yellow blouse dark with blood and bullet holes, her long black hair lying in the gutter at the edge of the street, her legs twisted at an unnatural angle.

With one stroke, my whole life had been destroyed.

How could I ever bring myself to accept it? Why shouldn't I be filled with anger and hatred for the men who did it — members of a drug gang who were just doing what they were told, men who had never been caught and never would be, protected by powerful politicians and wealthy godfathers, men who profited from the misery they caused? Why shouldn't I burn with hatred for such people?

But such was not the way of a Buddhist, and I knew it. Hatred did not cease by hatred, the Lord Buddha had said, but by love only, and sometimes that love was very costly indeed.

I was tired now, tired of carrying this burden. I was sorry my wife and son had died. I was sorry for what I had lost. I was sorry that I couldn't share life with them anymore. I was sorry I wasn't able to protect them that day, that I hadn't even thought they might be in danger.

But I needed to live. I needed to find a way to start loving other people again. I needed to find a way to be here, in this moment, in this reality, not lost in the past, grieving over what had happened years ago.

Thammarato appeared in the doorway of his kuti.

"You here to murder me, Ananda?" he asked, offering a yawn and a smile.

I had roused him from his afternoon nap.

"I need to talk," I said.

He went back into his kuti to fetch two glasses and a pitcher of water, which he brought out and sat on the porch. He sat down, cross-legged, sipping from a glass of water, and seemed perfectly awake, perfectly alert, not at all annoyed that I had roused him. He was, I thought, the closest thing to a Buddha that I was ever likely to see in my lifetime, and I was grateful that he was my friend.

"Having a hard time again?" he asked, giving me a knowing look.

"I'm ready to quit now," I said quietly. "But I don't know how."

For a long while we regarded each other in silence. I remained standing, sipping from the water he had given me. He remained sitting.

"Tell me, Ananda, do you ever cry about how painful it was to be born, when you had to leave your mother's womb and come into this world?"

I didn't understand what this might have to do with anything, but I knew Brother Thammarato was leading me into something or other, as was his way, getting me to go along while he made connections that eventually began to make sense the deeper one got into it.

"Of course not," I said. "I don't even remember that pain."

"You don't?" he asked, his eyes going wide, as if with astonishment. "There you were, all safe in your mother's womb, all your needs taken care of, no problems to speak of, and suddenly you're being forced to leave. It must have been shocking, upsetting — you must have been furious! What was she doing? Why wouldn't she let you stay? And after you made your way down that tunnel and out into the world, it must have been cold and frightening.

And then, as if to add insult to injury, they cut the umbilical cord that had been giving you food and sustenance. You must have been very angry indeed."

I smiled. I didn't remember any of this — who did?

He put a hand on his knee and regarded me as if I were a naughty school boy who wasn't being very honest with him. "Now, when you were a boy, did your father go off to work?"

I nodded.

"I see," he said. "And you probably wanted him to stay home and play with you and have fun."

That was true.

"So you must have been really angry about his leaving you every day, going off to work, leaving you at home with your mother. You're probably still angry about that, aren't you?"

"No," I said. "Why should I be?"

"Why shouldn't you be?" he demanded. "He left you, abandoned you, every day. Did he care about your feelings? Did he care about how boring it was for you to be home all day? Oh no, he was too busy. He was too important to be bothered with your little boredom. That doesn't make you angry? And what about all those fights you got into with the other boys, your brothers and sisters, all those scraped knees, broken bones, beatings, falling out of trees, who knows what? Aren't you angry about those things?"

I shook my head, seeing where he was going.

He regarded me for a long time. "I see," he said, now nodding his head. "So when it comes to past pains and hurts and wounds, you choose to cling to just certain ones, don't you, the more exciting ones. You can't be bothered with the little things. You go right for the big things."

"But it's different," I said defensively.

"Is it?" he asked. "Tell me, Ananda, if one of your boys came up to you and was crying about how painful it had been to be born, how scared he was, how cold it was, how mad he was because he mother had forced him to leave her body — if one of these boys came up to you and started complaining about that, what would you say to him? Doesn't he have a right to be angry? Wasn't it a painful, traumatic experience?"

I didn't answer, merely lowered my eyes. Part of me wanted pity, wanted people to feel sorry for me, to agree with me about how awfully I had been treated, how unfair life had been.

We all experienced the pain of being born. And we all experience the pain of death, of being separated from loved ones, of preparing for our own.

"All those childhood things, those hurts and pains," Thammarato said, "where are they now? Do you still think about them? Are you still mad about them? Are you still bitter, lusting for revenge? Or didn't you, like all of us, forget about them because there were more important things to do, there was life to live, there were new experiences, new things waiting around the corner?"

"You're saying I should forget about my wife and son?" I asked, some of my temper flaring.

"In a way, yes," he said. "You've been clinging to them, nursing your wounds, keeping it all fresh in your mind. Has it brought them back? Have you made yourself happy by doing that? Has it made it easier for you? Has it brought you peace and contentment?"

It certainly had not.

"So yes," he said, "I'm telling you to forget about it. Put it out of your mind. Remember the good things, of course, and take courage from them. Remember how they loved you, and how you loved them. Remember the happiness you had. Of course. But there has to come a point when you accept what happened to them, when you accept the fact of their deaths, accepting reality as it is. Their karma has taken them on to their next lives. Your karma has left you here, to cope with their loss. You will never be able to forget them — they are part of your life. They are part of who you are. If you hadn't met that woman, and if the two of you hadn't had that child, you wouldn't be the person who's standing here today. So of course, you can't forget them, and never will. But you have to let them die, Ananda. Each one of us is going to die. It has to be accepted. When you love someone, you don't want that person to die, but that's not going to stop it. There's nothing we can do about it. You've been bitter and angry about that for all these years, but has it helped you? Have you exhausted it now? Are you ready to let it go? When are you going to be human like the rest of us, and cry like a baby — have yourself a good sob — and then get on with it? What do you think the rest of us do, Ananda? Are you the only ones who has ever been hurt before?"

I stared at the ground. I knew what he was saying, the truth of it. I was creating my own suffering. Ultimately, no matter what happens to us, we can make choices about how we respond. We can be bitter and angry, or we can accept it and move on. We can cling to the past or embrace the future.

There was no easy solution to some of life's problems, no magic words, no waving of wands and presto! — instant cure. No. It didn't work that way. Reality had to be accepted the way it was. When that reality was pleasant, it was easy to do. But when it was ugly and painful, it wasn't so easy to do. And yet there was nothing else to do but accept it, and move on, accept it and let it be what it was.

I sat down on the steps to his kuti and for the first time in many years, I cried.

"Let it out, Ananda," Thammarato said. "Let it all out. It's like the Lord Buddha said: There is suffering. But don't forget what he said after that — There is an end to suffering."

And just then, the rains, which had been threatening to come for so long now, finally made their appearance, sending down a torrent of huge drops and darkening the sky. I moved up to the top step of Thammarato's kuti, miserable, wiping at my eyes and feeling embarrassed. The rains pounded down on the roofs of the kutis, on the grounds. The sound of it was loud, and yet somehow soothing.

I put my face in my hands and cried for a long time. Thammarato put his hand on my back and patted it, and the feeling of it, the simplicity of simple human contact, was comforting.

Life would go on, with me or without me. My wife and son had died, but I had not, and I had to go on living. It's what they would have wanted. And now, after so many years of grieving, it's what I wanted too.

I got hold of myself, wiping at my eyes, feeling both better and worse.

It was coming up on 4 p.m., and I had a meditation class to conduct for young boys who were probably in a lot more pain than I was.

"Thank you," I said to Thammarato, offering him a wai of respect and appreciation.

I saw an umbrella coming down the walkway, one of the boys beneath it. It stopped at Thammarato's kuti, and the face below it revealed itself — Yai.

"Father Ananda? Kittisaro sent me to find you. It's time for your class."

"It looks like I've got things to do," I said to Thammarato, and he smiled.

I darted down the stairs and under Yai's umbrella.

###

Nick Wilgus lived and worked in Asia for many years. Titles in his Father Ananda murder-mystery series, which include *Mindfulness and Murder*, *Garden of Hell* and *Killer Karma*, have been translated into French, German, Spanish and Italian.

An award-winning movie based on *Mindfulness and Murder* was released in 2011 by DeWarenne Pictures in Bangkok and nominated for Best Screenplay by the Thailand National Films Awards 2012.

Wilgus, who is also the author of *The Man Who Got Lost,* was recently named best general columnist by the Mississippi Press Association.

He lives in Seattle's Chinatown district..

'The Devil's Road To Kathmandu' by Tom Vater is a tense, fast paced and kaleidoscopic pulp thriller, following the lives of two generations of drifters who become embroiled in a saga of sex, drugs and murder on the road between London and the Indian subcontinent.

In 1976, four friends, Dan, Fred, Tim and Thierry, drive a bus along the hippy trail from London to Kathmandu. En Route in Pakistan, a drug deal goes badly wrong, yet the boys escape with their lives and the narcotics. Thousands of kilometers, numerous acid trips, accidents, nightclubs and a pair of beautiful Siamese twins later, as they finally reach the counter-culture capital of the world, Kathmandu, Fred disappears with the drug money.

A quarter century later, after receiving mysterious emails inviting them to pick up their share of the money, Dan, Tim and Thierry are back in Kathmandu. The Nepalese capital is not the blissful mountain backwater they remember. Soon a trail of kidnapping and murder leads across the Roof of the World. With the help of Dan's backpacking son, a tattooed lady and a Buddhist angel, the ageing hippies try to solve a 25-year old mystery that leads them amongst Himalayan peaks for a dramatic showdown with their past.

"The Devil's Road to Kathmandu is a better backpacker's book than The Beach."
The Bangkok Post

Cambodia 2001 - a country re-emerges from a half century of war, genocide, famine and cultural collapse.

German Detective Maier travels to Phnom Penh, the Asian kingdom's ramshackle capital to find the heir to a Hamburg coffee empire.

As soon as the private eye and former war reporter arrives in Cambodia, his search for the young coffee magnate leads into the darkest corners of the country's history and back in time, through the communist revolution to the White Spider, a Nazi war criminal who hides amongst the detritus of another nation's collapse and reigns over an ancient Khmer temple deep in the jungles of Cambodia.

Maier, captured and imprisoned, is forced into the worst job of his life – he is to write the biography of the White Spider, a tale of mass murder that reaches from the Cambodian Killing Fields back to Europe's concentration camps – or die.

"The narrative is fast-paced and the frequent action scenes are convincingly written. The smells and sounds of Cambodia are vividly brought to life, and aficionados of this kind of writing will love the book."

Crime Fiction Lover Blog

Down and out Luke and high-class Tara, linked intimately by a violent incident in London's seedy King's Cross, run away to the Philippines to escape their sordid pasts. But the tropics can be unkind to kids on the lam. On a remote island in the South China Sea they soon face more trouble than they can handle – with each other and the local criminal elements. Only a mysterious Englishman with a luxurious dive boat can spring them from their new predicament, with an offer of high seas adventure that has to be too good to be true. But Luke and Tara are in no position to refuse…

Crime Wave Press is a Hong Kong based fiction imprint that endeavors to publish the best new crime novels from Asia and about Asia to readers around the globe.

Founded in 2012 by acclaimed publisher Hans Kemp of Visionary World and seasoned writer Tom Vater, **Crime Wave Press** publishes a range of crime fiction – from whodunits to Noir and Hardboiled, from historical mysteries to espionage thrillers, from literary crime to pulp fiction, from highly commercial page turners to marginal texts exploring Asia's dark underbelly.

Crime Wave Press promotes strong voices, exceptional talent and unique points of view in the crime fiction genre.

Visit our website: http://www.crimewavepress.com
Follow us on Facebook: http://www.facebook.com/CrimeWavePress

CPSIA information can be obtained
at www.ICGtesting.com
Printed in the USA
LVHW091341030119
602624LV00001B/91/P